Near Perfect
GETAWAY

Claude Touchette

FriesenPress

Suite 300 - 990 Fort St
Victoria, BC, V8V 3K2
Canada

www.friesenpress.com

Copyright © 2017 by Claude Touchette
First Edition — 2017

All rights reserved.

No part of this publication may be reproduced in any form, or by any means, electronic or mechanical, including photocopying, recording, or any information browsing, storage, or retrieval system, without permission in writing from FriesenPress.

ISBN
978-1-4602-9488-8 (Paperback)
978-1-4602-9489-5 (eBook)

1. FICTION, CRIME

Distributed to the trade by The Ingram Book Company

October 31, 1952, Halloween night in the small county of Hillier Ontario and it's party time! Jeff and Bob Thorton, born twins, they had great parents in their 70's. Jeff lived with them. Bob had a farm, approximately 100 acres 2 miles from town. Jeff called Bob to see if he would go to a party with his wife. Bob said yah "its ok, we will go" and hung up the phone. Around 9pm they met at the local hall, all dressed up for Halloween. The dance started at 9:30pm and they were drinking pretty heavily. Jeff asked Bob, "Hey! What do you think of my new girlfriend Sylvia? Isn't she pretty?" Bob answered, "Yes she is, introduce me." As they began to trot and swagger toward Sylvia, Bob noticed she was dressed from head to toe in a black Patton leather cat suit which caressed each and every curve of her body, which ended in 6 inch heels and accompanied by a whip which made him think her part time job involved the expertise of a dominatrix. This thought brought Bob to a chuckle. Jeff introduced, "Bob this is Sylvia, Sylvia this is Bob." Bob says, "Can I dance with her?" Jeff replies, "Yes, go ahead." They began to dance to the Red River Polka. As their feet began to move Bob commented on Syliva's dancing styling. "I wish my wife would dance like that." Bob continued as he watched her move in the light. Sylvia immediately inquired to the whereabouts of his Bob's wife. Bob nervously said, "She is right over there. Would you like to meet her?"

As the introductions began within the small group of future friends, Bob, Jeff, Sylvia and Katie found it difficult to distinguish who was who with all the naughty costumes as far as the eye can see. Sylvia and Katie began their friendship with simple pleasantries. Sylvia introduced herself to Katie asking if she is enjoying the night. Katie replied "Yes, but I am sort of the quiet type, I like to watch." After a couple of dances with Bob, Sylvia suggested she should turn her attention back to Jeff. Sylvia noticed the linger in Bob's eyes was more than just a new friend look. They both went their separate ways to couple with their significant others they began their night with. Jeff and Sylvia had a few more cocktails as the clock struck midnight. Jeff suggested that perhaps they spend the night at a motel down the road as the fog began to roll in with a rain storm flooding the roads. This thought made Jeff nervous to drive with a couple cocktails under his belt. Let's tell the truth; his mind was focused on one thing and one thing only, a woman, privacy and a bed, not necessarily in that order. Sylvia did not have to convince herself to spend the night with Jeff, her thoughts surrounded the idea he was a very attractive man and a great catch. Immediately, both understood silently what was going to happen next, they departed from the party but not before they said their polite good-byes to Katie and Bob. Sylvia felt compelled to give her friend Melanie a ride home. Jeff said, "No problem, she only lives a short distance away." Once to the car, Jeff began to kiss Sylvia playfully. First on the cheek, then slowly moving down to her neck, sweet, soft, his hands began to wander. Her virginity flashing before her eyes as he caresses her breasts, hips and then on top of her cat suit feels the upper area of her thigh. Sylvia's eyes close and she breaths out slowly. The rain appeared to be fuelling the eroticism rushing through both of their veins. Jeff found the cat suit unnecessary and in his mind needs to be removed as quickly as possible. Knock. Knock. Sylvia abruptly grabbed Jeff's wrists to hold him back; this was going too far for the atmosphere. Sylvia proclaimed to Jeff they had to get Melanie home because she was patiently waiting in the car. As they entered the vehicle, to their disbelief, they were amazed by her behaviour Melanie was masturbating, what a shock! This occurrence made Jeff and Sylvia, even more, sexually aroused. Jeff's hands began to wander again over Sylvia's body. His hands grasped her face as he kissed her with steaming passion. Jeff said "Honey, you are the most beautiful girl in the world and I can't help myself. You are really turning me on." Sylvia giggled like a school girl and told Jeff to drive. As Jeff pulled onto the road the rain began to really come down. The visibility was limited and the cocktails began to take effect. Jeff turned around to the back seat and said to Melanie, "Honey, you will be home in a minute." Sylvia moved closer and closer as Jeff continued to drive. Her right hand found its way to the inside of his right thigh. She explored the unknown as she noticed his penis was beginning to enlarge. The unknown was intriguing to her as a virgin. She cupped his manhood feeling the outline, rubbing and caressing, shocked by the increasing size of his penis. "Oh my god, this is big! It's hard as a rock!" Jeff turned and just smiled, no words, just a smile. Jeff turned to Sylvia and said, "Honey, it's about to explode, you have to take it easy. The roads are slippery; you have to hold on until we get to the motel. Ok Sweet?" Sylvia was persistent in her actions. She wanted to continue to play with the unknown sexual pleasures of life, it was fun. "I promise it won't hurt my darling." She said. Fifty miles an hour the car raced down the road in limited visibility. Finally they reached Melanie's house. Melanie shot out of the car to get out of the rain as quickly as possible.

Here we go! A night of passion ahead. They were a mile from the motel and the road was becoming more slick, multiple curves coming up so Jeff decided to slow down a little but Sylvia could not restrain her animal passion. Jeff's mind became more blurry as the minutes continued. All of a sudden he saw an oncoming car around the curve, swerving, losing control. Jeff was too late to avoid side swiping the oncoming car. They came to a screeching halt 100 feet away from the swerving car. Jeff looked at Sylvia and screamed, "Ah Shit! Where did he go?" Sylvia did not let go of Jeff, she continued to hang on to his big knob. They realized that the other car went over the embankment into the lake. Sylvia panicked and insisted they turn around and investigate. Her hand not removing from the position it began, on his manhood. Jeff said to Sylvia, "Let go of my penis and we will turn the car around to see!" As they were driving back, Sylvia noticed tracks. "Stop! You can see where it went over the embankment." They pulled over. "Jeff, it is too deep, I can't see the car! You got a flashlight?" Jeff reached over to the glove compartment and retrieved the flashlight. "Thanks" Sylvia replied. Sylvia investigated with the assistance of the flashlight. "I can't see the car Jeff! It is just water. What should we do? Jeff, I'm scared, I can't see the car" At that point they turned, headlights in the distance, coming around the corner. Jeff threw himself into the middle of the road violently waving the car down. It happened to be a police cruiser. As the police officer strutted out of the cop car thinking to find two young kids drunk or high out of their minds, he found Sylvia and Jeff, frantic over the car in the lake. The cop took a look and could not see a car. The police officer decided to pull his car closer to the embankment and hook up a rope to the back. Jeff held it to ensure the safety of the police man as he made his way, climbing, down. It was a 25 foot drop straight down to the edge of the lake. The officer yelled to Jeff that he could see the car submerged under approximately 15 feet of water. The officer instructed Jeff to use his radio and call for assistance. Jeff followed the instructions given to him by the officer. The officer already knew that the victims did not get out of the car. It was about 30 minutes after the initial crash. There were no air bubbles, no sign of life and no bodies floating around the water. There was little hope of survival. Jeff and Sylvia were visibly shaking from the trauma of the night and the wet cold atmosphere. Sylvia continued to panic as she turned to Jeff asking, "What are we going to do?" Jeff said, "I don't know what the police will do but we have to stay calm and collected, we can't let them know we have been drinking." It took approximately 45 minutes for another two cruisers and a tow truck to arrive at the crash scene. There was also a trained officer in diving gear. The tow truck was placed in position, backed up to the embankment, the wench and hook was lowered down the embankment. The experienced officers followed suit, diving into the lake to hook the submerged car by the back axel. "Start pulling her up!" The tow truck began to wench the car out. As the car was hauled out of the lake water began to pour out slowly. Silence spread over all watching, there was two adults bodies, suspected in their mid 40's in the front seat and one small child, a little girl presumed the daughter around 10 or 12, in the back seat. No one was wearing seat belts, they could only imagine the frantic feeling in each of the victims as the water began to fill the car, scrambling to get their restraints off and breathe the air of safety. As the final drops left the car each participant continued to do all they could while the vehicle was pulled up the 25 foot steep embankment. The officers concluded to leave the bodies in the vehicle until they could transport the car to the nearest police compound for further investigation. Two officers on the road decided to question the only witnesses involved in this accident. Jeff was being questioned on what their roll was in this situation. The officers could smell alcohol on his breathe. Red flags began to pop up. "Due to the circumstances sir we have to ask you to take a breathalyser test." Jeff said to one of the police officers "I am not drunk. What do you want this for?" Jeff responded. Due to the shock of what Jeff saw this dark night he appeared to be more sober than what he really was. The officer responded, "We have a triple homicide and we do need a test. We can do this the easy way or the hard way. Your choice!" Nervously, "If I have too then fine. What do I do?" Jeff said. The officer grabbed the breathalyser machine and instructed him to blow hard. Jeff proceeded to blow hard into the machine. The reading went from 0.05, 0.08 to 1.05, he was two times over the legal limit. "We will have to take you to the station for a secondary test." The officer commanded forcefully. Jeff tried to talk his way out of going to the station but no chance. He knows he is in trouble, deep trouble. Sylvia tried her best to comfort Jeff as they cuffed him and threw him in the back of the cop car. Sylvia was also apprehended and put into a separate cop car for the transportation to the Police Station. In the mean time they towed the car to Picton for

ID's on the bodies and further investigation. Select officers remained to conduct the crime scene investigation, analyzing skid marks they noticed on the road. The Officer in charge after reading the breathalyser test charged Jeff with impaired driving and homicide. Sylvia was released following her interrogation at the station with no charges laid. Sylvia was allowed to say her goodbyes to Jeff, "I will see you in the morning." Jeff was then booked, processed and put behind bars pending the conclusion of the investigation. Jeff was allowed his one phone call. He called his brother Bob. "Hey Bob. There was a terrible accident, I am involved in it, Sylvia was with me." Bob interjected, "Is Sylvia ok?" "Yes, she has gone home. Can I see you?" Jeff replied. "OK, I will come first thing in the morning and see if I can get you out, I will try and get money together to post bail. Try and get some sleep. OK? You can explain to me in the morning exactly what happened." Bob went to bed, his wife Kathy sensed something was wrong. "What happened Bob? What's wrong?" Bob explained, "Jeff had an accident, I will look after it in the morning. He is in jail right now." Katie would not drop the inquiry about the accident. "Is Jeff ok? Is Sylvia ok? Why is Jeff in jail?" Bob let her know that both were fine, a couple scratches but nothing serious. Sylvia was sent home, you can call her tomorrow when I go to the station to see Jeff. I don't know anything else so go back to sleep." Bob could not sleep. He did not have the answers he needed about the situation. He paced around the floors for hours wondering how bad this situation is. The sun began to rise Bob jumped back into bed for a couple minutes of shut eye but no luck. Jeff did not sleep at all, those jail cells are not very comfortable. Six am Bob jumped out of bed, fuelled himself with coffee and toast. Katie asked Bob if she could go with him to the station. "No it is better if I go by myself." Bob replied. Bob left for town, arriving around 8:30am, right to the jail house hoping they would let him see Jeff. Upon arrival the officer condoned the visit however placed a 30 minute restraint on the visit. The officer also disclosed to Bob that Jeff was to appear in court at 10am. "You will have to probably arrange bail." Bob went in and gave Jeff a big hug, "Jeff, you look tired. Not much sleep eh?" Bob said jokingly. Jeff responded nervously, "I had a terrible night, one for the books. I don't know what I am going to do Bob. Three people are dead. They are going to through away the keys. You have to help me out. You are my twin brother; I only have you to rely on. PLEASE.?!" Bob insisted, "I will not leave you stuck, that's a promise. Time's up. I will see you in court." Now it is ten o'clock, time for the bail hearing. Bob stood in court to ask the judge for release of Jeff on his own recognisance. The judge refused at first due to the severity of the case. Because of the good family name he relented and set the bail at $5000. The trial date was set for November 28, 1952. Bob then swiftly went to his parents for the money. The parents were not aware of the situation with Jeff yet. When Bob told them it was just about enough to kill them. Their parents were in their late 70's and in no condition to deal with these kids. Bob proceeded to tell them that he would do everything in his power to get Jeff off of all charges.

The following morning, the bodies were identified as a Wayne Cartwright, farmer from approximately 5 miles from out of town, his wife Joan and their 5 year old daughter Dorothy. Only one son remained alive, John 18 years of age. John patiently waiting at home for his family to arrive awoke by a knocking at the door. Two Police Officers stood at attention upon the front porch. "John Cartwright? I have some disturbing news. Tonight there was a horrific accident. Your parents and sister have been killed in a car accident close to the lake on Highway 33." John fell to his knees sobbing. One officer, which had a little boy just around the age of John immediately, bent down to pick him off the floor. "I know what a shock this is, you will get through this." After the shock and sadness consumed John the officers insisted he come with them and identify the bodies. "No! I can't do that. I don't want to see them dead. This can't be happening." With tears in his eyes, the officer said, "You must." John gathered his personal items and went with the officers for the long ride in the cruiser. Once reaching the hospital morgue John's knees became weak. One officer on his left and the other on his right, holding him up as he walked into his future. John noticed everything that morning. The crisp air, fog dissipating, the trees blowing in the wind, and the colors of the ever changing leaves. The hospital corridors appeared empty, cold, dead. He felt a chill as he walked, he had no idea where he was going however knew each and every step as though it was familiar. Now the morgue door, half glass and still cold. The door swung open as the mortician came to great his guests. You know he does not really have many guests with a pulse. As John's had turned to the left he saw the wall of slab drawers which held the dead. The eerie feeling rushed over him making his hairs on his arms stand on end. Tears did not come to his eyes; he was filled with so much shock of the situation. The mortician began to pull on a drawer handle. Slowly he revealed a black body bag. Who was it? Was it his mother? Was it his sister? Or was it dad? As he heard the slow unzipping of the body bag he saw the outline of his father's face. Flashes of light came to his mind. Fishing trips and hunting events flashed before him, just memories. John, with no tears, said "That is my dad, Wayne Cartwright." The mortician moved closer to John pulling out another drawer as the one previous was now sealed closed. The sound of the zipper in his ears once again. It was his mother. Her hair as red as fire, her skin as white as a ghost, however her beauty still remain. "That's my mom." John said with no expression. The third drawer began to open and the second shut closed. He knew what he was going to see. A big deep breathe. The zipper sound again, this time louder. It was her, small meek, gentle, a simple child lost in death. John dropped to his knees and began to sob like a baby. He yelled, "Not her, anyone but her." The bond was unmistakable. John and Joan were close; they did everything together, living on a farm. From chores to playing in the yard, yelling and screaming as they ran through the sprinkler in the middle of the hot summer days. John could not contain himself, there was no control, and he was like a broken man at the age of 18. The officers grabbed John to pull him to his feet, trying to console him in any way possible. In their minds John was a young man now forced to face the world on his own. In true form, the officers began to ask John if he would like to go to relatives instead of going home to an empty house.

Jeff was now out on bail, the conditions were specified as not able to leave the township of Hillier without notifying the police. This was not a condition of bail he was going to take lightly. Bob travelled home to try to explain to his wife the situation, a lot of arguments ensued with his wife over Jeff's legal issues. As a result their love life suffered. They began to sleep in separate beds, avoid each other's gaze, they began to grow apart. November 20, 1952, the leaves have already fallen, weather drops drastically in the night air, the ground cold and hard, light snow on the horizon and now before them is the court date. Bob made a trip to assure his parents the court date has arrived and everything was going to work out. Little did he know when he arrived at the house they grew up in his dad was not well, frail and weak, he did not appear healthy. His mother pleaded with him to take his father to the hospital. The three of them drove to the hospital, mom in the back and father in the front. The tears began to fall as Bob's mother wept for her husband's well-being. In her eyes he might not make it. This hospital visit ended in a potentially long term stay. His heart was weak and failing, any day his situation could result in a heart attack. The doctor came to both Bob and his mother with the disturbing news. Bob's father could not take any more stress, any more pain. This worried Bob and deterred him from consoling his parents with his worries for Jeff. Bob helped his mother into the car. On the drive back to his parent's house he said to his mother, "Mom, I have to go back to Katie, you know how some women can be." Instead of going home Bob decided to go for a little thinking time. Bob was not a drinker however he loved to have a drink. After he dropped his mother off at home he went to the local pub to have a couple drinks. One drink turned into a couple more, a couple more turned into many more, he decided that one more could not hurt. As to his surprise, Lindsay, an old school mate struts into the bar and recognised Bob from his old school days. And still single at that. She was around 32, 5' 7" tall with blonde hair, blue eyes, and beautiful shape, nice firm boobs, dressed in a slinky tight sweater, nipples pushing through. She came in sat herself in the stool next to Bob. "Bob? I have not seen you in years! How long has it been? Ten years? How have you been keeping? Are you married? Any kids?" Bob replied half in the bag, slurring his words, "I remember you. Lindsay, right? I could be better. How have you been?" Lindsay sensed Bob had problems that were not going to be cured by just a few drinks. She moved closer to him, so close she could feel his breath. Her left hand moved closer to his right thigh. She looked into his eyes and said, "If you have a problem you can talk to me." Bob said under his breath, "Well honey, I have been through a lot of shit and I am just trying to forget about it." "Just talk to me, Maybe I can help" Lindsay said. Even as she said that she got even closer, her hand moving up his thigh. Now Bob starts to notice and feel her movement. Naturally, Bob began to forget about his problems, his mind preoccupied. He was fighting with his wife, no sex at home so he began to think about the soft curves of Lindsay's body. How would it feel to touch her? How would it feel to slip it inside? His nuts felt like they were going to explode. He notices an inkling in the nether region. Lindsay suggests to him that perhaps he has had too much to drink and perhaps they would be able to go back to her place, not too far from there, to hang out and talk. However that was not Lindsay's intentions. As they walked down the street, Bob bouncing from one street poll to the next, they each stole a kiss or two. Each kiss became more passionate as each step was taken. Her red lips called out for him. As the door swung open Bob grabbed Lindsay's hips, pulled her in and kissed her, pulled her hair to extend her neck, like a vampire he could not get enough of her. They travelled down the long narrow hallway and he began, like a savage to pull off her clothes. She grabbed him around the neck, jumped and wrapped her legs around him. She could feel the bulge in his pants. "Where is your bedroom?" Bob yelled. "Over there!" Lindsay pointed in a direction Bob could not see. He had a few drinks so he was not the most stable on his feet. He almost dropped her a couple times so he decided to let her walk. Well no, that was not going to happen so soon. He pinned her up against the wall, both hands above her head. She could not move, she was not in control, he was. A little slap on the ass made her even more excited. With the blood rushing through their veins they finally made it to the bed. With hands free Lindsay pushes him on the chest to make him fall onto the bed. As he fell back she was already undoing his top button on his shirt. She moved from button to button until she was able to spread his shirt wide open exposing his chest; then his pants. The top button popped off due to the ever increasing size of the bulge in his pants. ZIP. There it is. The shaft of glory. She did not want to hurt him so she reached down his boxers. Gripping his large shaft in her small hands made her feel powerful. She was in control this time. Poor Lindsay was so ready to receive the shaft of love she became so wet and pussy became so tight like a clam at sea. Since Bob had not had sex in quite a while, as she started to play with his penis, he blew his fucking load. Disappointment of no satisfaction filled Lindsay; it was really unfortunate it was the only thing that filled her. Bob began to sober up after blowing his load and he realized how beautiful her body was as she lay there naked beside him. His dick began to get hard again and she did not give up easily. She began to play with him 5 minutes later. Bob being quite a man began to become hard again in no time. He could not hold back the animal instinct came out. As Lindsay laid on her back he grabbed her by the top of the legs and pulled her into him. He entered her with conviction. The power and force of him entering her made Lindsay yell out. The fire burning inside her, She could not help but to have one of the best climaxes she has ever had. It was pure ecstasy. Lindsay and Bob were so tired after the sexual events they fell asleep completely satisfied. They woke several hours later and thought they were in some fantasy island somewhere in the Pacific. Many hours after continuous foreplay they decided to go their separate ways by sneaking out of the motel room one at a time. No one could catch them, Bob has a wife. As Bob sobered he wanted to focus on what was most important, his brother Jeff and his family. Bob quickly jumped into his vehicle and sped off to visit his mother and father.

As he arrived at the house he found his mother and Jeff sitting on the front porch discussing his father's current health situation. Bob approached them with a quick and mysterious "Hello", trying to hide all the wrong doing he was just involved in minutes before. He continued to further inquire about his father, "Have you been updated on Dad's condition?" His mother abruptly inquired on his whereabouts the night previous, "Where have you been? Where were you all night? We went to go visit your father and you were nowhere to be found. Your wife has been calling here looking for you." Bob replied, "I was troubled, I went to the bar and had a few drinks, thought I shouldn't drive so I spent the night sleeping in my car." Suddenly the front door swung open and Julia said with a smirk, "Yah, right!" She was fourteen years old with long blonde hair and blue eyes. The conversation was then abruptly dropped. Bob then asked Jeff to accompany him on a walk. They said to the ladies they would be back shortly. As they walked out into the field Bob turned to Jeff to discuss the tactics for trial. They must stick to the same story even though the cops have all of the evidence and they don't know which way this trial going to go. "OK Jeff, let's start by going over all the evidence the cops have collected and what happened leading up to the car accident." Bob said nervously. Jeff just nodded in silence. "OK. OK. So this is what happened. The oncoming car came around the curve on Highway 33 right by Conscecon, they seemed they were losing control and swerving across the solid white line. Remember in the rain? It happened so fast, I am sure we were on our side of the road. That is when the car did lose control and sideswiped our car causing them to drive over the embankment and into the water. By the time we stopped, reversed and got out of the car their vehicle was already submerged. We could not find it anywhere, it was gone, disappeared. That night we were at Barhaven dancing, we only had five drinks each over the duration of four hours. We were not intoxicated; you were able to drive just fine. And that is the fucking story we are going to stick too. Alright? Did you hear me?" Jeff continued to nod his head in agreement. No words, just nodding. "You got this Jeff! You can do this! I will be right there beside you. I will not leave you. I will do anything in my power to get you through this." Bob yelled as he grabbed his brother's shoulders and stared him right in the eyes. Nothing more to be said, they turned and walked back to the house. As they arrived they found their mother and Julia, their sister, getting ready to leave and visit their father in the hospital. They collected their personal items and piled into the car. The entire family was going to sit by father's bed in support. As they entered the hospital they could feel the cold sterile air. Was it foreshadowing of what was to come? As they took each step towards their fathers hospital room Jeff began to become more nervous, he began to sweat. They walked in all together to see their father lying in bed, dark circles around his eyes, skin more wrinkled then they remember, tubes running under the blanket and a pretend smile on his face. They were his children coming in and Doug had to put on a face, trying to let them know he was going to be fine. His arms reached out to hug Julia as she ran to her father's side. "I love you!" He whispered in her ear. "You look beautiful! You are the most beautiful girl I have ever seen." Julia instantly said, "Bull shit dad, Mom is the most beautiful girl you have ever seen." The doctor made an appearance, first extending a greeting to Doug's family then picking up his chart. The doctor said, "I am glad your entire family is here. I have the results from the tests and it is not that bad of news. You have a bad heart. Now, we might be able to control this illness with a bunch of pills and you may be able to go home soon. You will not be able to do any strenuous exercise however you will be able to live comfortably doing normal daily things such as reading the paper, going to town to do shopping, you know things like that." Doug was immediately worried due to the fact that he had a farm to take care of. Who would he rely on to get the work done? Well, I guess that is one thing that will remain on his mind. The main focus is to get better and go home. The family said their good-byes and made their way down to the car with at least decent news of their father's health. Back at the farm Julia went to go play and the three adults began to speak of the trial. They did not want to stress out their father by discussing the upcoming trail at the hospital.

Jeff likes to drink and is so stressed he could use a beer. The three of them had a couple beers and spoke of everyday life trying to forget about the events to come. A couple days quietly passed at the house awaiting the trial.

Trial, November28th, 1952, 10am. The court house was packed, not a seat to find so there were even people standing to witness the outcome of the trial. Defendant's lawyer was in place, the prosecutor also awaiting the judge and juries arrival. The jury was made up of thirteen people who were pre-selected before the trial date. It appeared to be a jury which would favor the defendant. The jury included a mixture of men and women from all social classes of the immediate society, teachers who live by a set of rules, farmers which would identify with the victims, and young adults that too would have a few drinks one night at a party and drive home. No one knew how they would decide after hearing the facts of the trial. The court clerk, once silent speaks, "Please rise. Judge Judy Patterson will be presiding in the case of Jeff Thorton the defendant verses the Crown in the death of Wayne, Joan and Dorothy Cartwright." The court clerk then motions to the crowd to have a seat. As Judge Judy Patterson takes her seat for what she knows is going to be a long court day, she grabs her gavel to begin the proceedings. "Please proceed with the Crowns case." Very confidently the Crown stood to make his opening statement. "Your honor, in the case of Jeff Thorton we find on October 31, 1952 he was driving erratically on a slick road under the influence of alcohol, he side swiped the deceased vehicle forcing them to veer off the road and over the embankment, at this time sending them to their watery graves. During these proceedings we will show you a series of scientific evidence which will support the charges of homicide. The defence now rises to counter the opening statement of the Crown. "Your honor we will present cut and dry evidence that the defendant was not intoxicated, was clearly sideswiped by the driver of the opposite vehicle and therefore the charges should be dropped.

The Defense began to open their case. "Your honor, at this time we would like to call the Lead Officer involved on October 31, 1952 to the stand." Out of the crowd a large man stood complete with uniform, his stature was tall, muscular, intimidating. He approached the stand ready with a file to refer too. The court clerk approached with a bible in hand asking the OPP Officer to place his left hand on the bible. As he did so the court clerk said "Please raise your right hand and swear to tell the truth, nothing but the truth, so help you God." The officer replied, "Yes". The court clerk continues, "You may sit down." The Judge gave the instructions to the Crown to approach the stand to proceed with their line of questioning. The Defense stood and approached the stand looking directly into the eyes of the OPP Officer.

Defense: "On the night of October 31, 1952 you were called to the scene in question, is that correct?"
Officer: "Correct."

Defense: "When you arrived at the scene, what did you see?"

Officer: "As I got out of the car I noticed the defendant and a women, later found to be a female escort of the defendant, standing looking over the embankment. "

Defense: "What were they looking at?"

Officer: "I asked them what seemed to be the problem. They told me that a car had side swiped them, lost control and disappeared over the embankment."

Defense: "What happened next?"

Officer: "I looked for the car and could not see it in in the water, everything was dark. I went to the car, opened the trunk and grabbed a rope, tied it around a tree and lowered myself down the 25 foot embankment to get a closer look. There I saw the car completely submerged and called up to the defendant to go to the police car and use the radio to call dispatch for further assistance." Soon, more police cars arrived and we got a police officer suited up to dive into the cold water in order to see if there was a chance for rescue. The diver went into the water, came back up about 7 minutes later and notified the rest of us the car was about 15feet from the water level and there were 3 bodies, one in the back seat and two in the front."

Defense: "Who were the victims?"

Officer: "At the time no names were known, however it appeared to be a man, a wife and a small child dead in the car. I sent for a tow truck to retrieve the car from the water. It took about 45 minutes to pull the car from the darkness."

Defense: "Did you speak with the individuals that were present at the scene?"

Officer: "Yes I did."

Defense: "What did you ask them? How did they appear?"

Officer: "When I approached the defendant he appeared to be nervous and upon his breathe I could smell alcohol. I asked him to describe in detail what happened to cause this accident. The defendant explained that they were driving home and the oncoming car was coming around the curve, losing control and side swiped him. They lost full control of the car and drove over the embankment."

Defense: ""Tell us about the investigation and your findings."

Officer: "We looked at the tracks on the road to verify the defendant's story, collected that night at the station during questioning, that the other vehicle side swiped him. It appears that the tire marks clearly show that the defendant's vehicle was on the left of the white line, west bound, as the other vehicle was headed east bound and must have been on their side of the road. By looking at the tire marks of the victim's vehicle, they remained on their side of the road until one point where there was a skid mark pulling them left and over the embankment.""

Defense: "Can you please further explain how you believe the tire marks of the defendant were his and not someone else's? Officer, what do you mean it appears the skid marks on the road indicated the victim's vehicle remained on their side of the road? Were they or weren't they? Do you have any photos or any other supporting evidence to substantiate this claim?"

Officer: "No, we went by visual assessment and documentation."

Defense: "Well, if you go by visual assessment how do you know these are not the tracks of another car not involved in this accident?"

Officer: "Well they were fresh tracks, they were just made. One would have to assume it would have to be their tracks."

As the Defense asked the questions he turned toward the jury to ensure they were all listening to the next answer.

Defense: "So, is it safe to say, if you did not take photos of tracks and you do not know 100% without a doubt these tracks belong to the defendant, there is no way you have the photos of the defendants tire thread to compare to the actual track marks visually seen at the scene?"

Officer: "No, I can't say we do. I can't say without a doubt they are his tire marks."

Defense: "Thank you for your honesty officer... Now can you tell me what kinds of cars were involved? What kind of car did the victim have? What kind of car was the defendant driving?"

Officer: "The victim's car was a Volkswagen Bug and the defendant's car was a 1946 Buick Electra."

Defense: "Wouldn't you think a little Volkswagen Bug if it were to impact a much larger car such as a 1946 Buick that the Volkswagen would not have bounced right off the Buick? Which would cause the Bug to go over the embankment? Do you think the heavy 1946 Buick would be moved on the road or hold his track?"

Officer: "As we conducted the investigation we did not find any tire marks over the white line at the impact point. So yes I do believe the weight of the Buick would hold up to the impact of a Volkswagen Bug."

Defense: "That is all the questions I have at this time, thank you your honor."

Judge: "Crown, at this time would you like to cross examine this witness?"

Crown: "Yes I would your honor."

During the entire testimony of the officer the Crown continued to take notes and pose questions to the officer in order to favor his cause.

Crown: "Officer, other than the tire marks on the road, is there anything else in the physical investigation that the good people of the police department were able to uncover?"

Officer: "Upon the investigation of the victims' vehicle we found that the marks were on the driver's side of the car, after the back door. This would make sense because of the skid marks on the road. As the defendant's car impacted the victims' vehicle it pushed the weight of the car creating it to fishtail, lose control and skid hard to the left and over the embankment."

Crown: "Just to clarify for the jury, the weight of the Buick would over power the weight of the victim's Volkswagen Bug causing it to lose control."

The Crown walked around the court room stargazing on his approach to the final questions for the witness.

Crown: "When you were speaking with the defendant at the scene of the accident, please tell the court if you noticed anything interesting. He was coming from a dance correct?"

Officer: "I did inquire how much the defendant had to drink that night; he said he only had 5beer over the entire duration for the night. The defendant tried to deny the breathalyser test first and then finally agreed."

Crown: "What was the result of the breathalyser?"

Officer: "He blew 1.05. The legal limit is 0.08."

The Defense suddenly interjects with "Objection your honor! The Crown assumes the defendant had an alcohol limit of 1.05, did anyone check the accuracy of this breathalyser machine? This is supposed to be hard evidence however you don't even know for sure if the machine is functioning properly. "

Crown: "Your honor, the defendant's blood alcohol limit is relevant that this is evidence. It is relevant to this case."

Judge: "How do we know which breathalyser was used to conduct the test with the defendant?"

Officer: "There is a serial number on our documentation of the investigation which will determine the machine used in this particular case."

Judge: "Request granted to the defense, the breathalyser will be sent to the lab and checked for its accuracy so we will know the integrity of the results by tomorrow's session."

Defense: "Thank you your honor."

Judge: "Crown, please proceed."

Crown: "I have no further questions your honor."

Judge: "This marks the end of the day people. Court is adjourned until 10am tomorrow morning. The jury will be sequestered to the motel for the duration of trial. Just a reminder to the jury, this case is not to be discussed with anyone or charges will be laid."

The defendant was escorted by the bailiff out of the court house first to deter anyone from trying to make a move on his life. Jeff was put into a car and driven to an unknown address for his safety.

November 29th, 1952 10am, the court was more filled with people than the day before. "Please rise. Judge Judy Patterson will be presiding in the case of Jeff Thorton the defendant verses the Crown in the death of Wayne, Joan and Dorothy Cartwright." The court clerk then motions to the crowd to have a seat. Immediately Judge Patterson motioned for the results of the breathalyser to be delivered to the bench. As she examined the results she asked,

Judge: "Can the Crown and Defense please approach the bench?"

As the gentleman approached the bench, Crown and Defense, the judge requested a brief recess for the two representatives to join her in her chambers. Once in her chambers, she closed the doors for complete privacy, being a liberal judge, "I know what time it is but I sure need a drink. You guys in for a little scotch?" Judge Patterson took off her robe and hung it up with care and respect. She poured three drinks not waiting for a response from either of the men, the largest for her of course. She sat down and put her feet up on her desk. "Well boys, I have read and understand the results of this examination pertaining to the breathalyser machine and I think you need to take a close look at to establish your cases." She handed the results to the Defense first. The Defense then handed the information to the Crown. The results made them both pick up their generous glasses of scotch, little did the judge know that both the Crown and the Defense were not Scotch drinkers and did not desire to be. They both felt the burning horrible taste of the Scotch as it went down sip by sip. The Crown then turned to the Judge began to laugh and said, "This is going to be a short day!" They collected themselves following the glass of double malt Scotch, took at mint and then proceeded back to the court room. Not a few minutes later as expected however 10 minutes later, after another drink, the Judge followed.

Court Clerk: "May the court rise? Judge Judy Patterson presiding."

The Judge took her seat and began the presiding's. The Judge noticed once she took position the Officer which was on stand the day before looked nervous, agitated, not knowing if he or the machine might have fucked up.

Judge: "Defense, your next witness."

Defense: "Yes your honor, I call Sylvia Tremblay to the stand."

Court Clerk: "Please raise your right hand and swear to tell the truth, nothing but the truth, so help you God."

Sylvia: "I do."

Defense: "On October 31, 1952, please tell us what you believe happened in your own words."

Sylvia looked the judge in the eyes and said,

Sylvia: "Your honor, we were driving home and there was a car coming towards us from around the corner. It seemed to be out of control, I saw it swerving, I was so scared, it happened so fast I really did not see much. All I know is that I heard the bang on the side of the car and as soon as they passed us I looked back and the car was no longer there. There were no tail lights. I yelled at Jeff to stop and we should turn around and go look."

Defense: "When you stopped, did Jeff help you look for the car?"

Sylvia: "Yes of course."

Defense: "When the police showed up, what happened?"

Sylvia: "The policeman went down the embankment attached to a rope, then called up to Jeff to use his radio and call for help. Once other police arrived I was removed from the area and put in a cop car."

Defense: "I have no further questions."

Judge: "Crown, would you like to cross examine?"

Crown: "No your honor."

Judge: "Defense, please call your next witness."

Defense: "I have no further witnesses to call."

Judge: "Crown, Please call your first witness."

Crown: "The Crown now calls the defendant to the stand, Jeff Thorton."

As Jeff nervously moved back his chair you could see his hands begin to shake. His thoughts overcame him. What was the outcome of the day going to be? He knew he had a few drinks, was it too much that night? Or was the machine not working properly? As he did so the court clerk said "Please raise your right hand and swear to tell the truth, nothing but the truth, so help you God." Jeff replied, "Yes". The court clerk continues, "You may sit down." The Judge gave the instructions to the

Crown to approach the stand to proceed with their line of questioning.

Defense: "In the night in question, October 31, 1952, to your recollection, how hard was it raining?"

Jeff: "Fairly hard."

Defense: "How would you describe the visibility?"

Jeff: "Very bad."

Defense: "How would you describe the weather? Was it raining?"

Jeff: "Yes."

Defense: "Was there fog?"

Jeff: "Yes."

Crown: "Where were you that night? Where were you coming from?"

Jeff: "I was coming from Barhaven, the Town Hall just outside of Consecon."

Crown: "What were you doing there?" Jeff: "That night they had a dance for Halloween."

Crown: "How much did you have to drink that night?"

Jeff: "I had a couple of drinks."

Crown: "What is a couple of drinks to you?"

Jeff: "I had three or four over the duration of the night."

Crown: "How long was the duration of the night before you left the hall?"

Jeff: "I was at the hall from about 9pm to 1pm, shortly before closing."

Crown: "So that was three drinks over the duration of four hours?"

Jeff: "Yes."

Crown: "Well Jeff, the breathalyser results have been established and the machine was working fine. You were gaged at 1.50 which would mean that you would have to have consumed many more than three or four drinks in the duration of four hours you said you were at the hall."

Jeff: "It didn't feel like I had that many drinks. I really think I had three or four drinks. I wasn't counting on how many I had."

Crown: "Legally you were drunk. The legal limit is 0.08. This means that you would have to of been below 0.08 to operate a vehicle safely."

Jeff: "I was fine to drive. What do you think I have a breathalyser in my dashboard?"

Judge: "Mr. Thorton, this is a serious case, people are dead, you are expected to answer the questions posed or I will hold you in contempt of court."

Jeff: "Yes your honor, I apologize deeply."

Judge: "Crown, if you have any further questioning please proceed."

Crown: "Thank you your honor. Jeff, after you hit the car, what did you do?"

Jeff: "Your honor, I did not hit the car, they side swiped me."

Crown: "Are you sure you did not cross the white line while driving as the officer stated yesterday?"

Jeff: "I am positive."

Crown: "How are you positive if you were impaired driving? You are not even positive on how many drinks you consumed that night."

Jeff: "I definitely saw the oncoming car swerving as it was approaching me, it happened so fast."

Crown: "Let's go to the point of after the impact. What happened?"

Jeff: "After the impact Sylvia turned around and said the car disappeared. She said she was not able to see the tail lights anymore. I said something along the lines of Oh Shit, we better go back. We pulled over and backed up to where we believed the car went over the embankment and could not see anything. That is when the police officer pulled up and asked us what the matter was. Why were we on the side of the road?"

Crown: "Why did you not just make a U-turn and go back? Why did you reverse down the road? Does that not tell you that you were not thinking properly and you were obviously impaired?"

Jeff: "I just saw a car go over the embankment. What would you have done?"

Judge: "Please adhere to the questioning, I have warned you once, I will not warn you again. Crown, please proceed."

Crown: "After the officer arrived, what did you do?"

Jeff: "I told him that I could not see the car, I told him we thought it had gone over the embankment and that is when the officer lowered himself down the embankment to get a closer look then called up to me to use his radio and call for help. I did as I was asked. More cops arrived. Sylvia was put into a cop car, I was put in another and then I was taken to the police station for further questioning. I am sure you have the records of my conversations at the station."

The judge looked at Jeff with the eyes to indicate, be careful.

The Judge: "Crown, do you have any more questions for the plaintiff?"

Crown: "No your honor."

Judge: "Defense, would you like to cross examine?"

Defense: "No your honor, we have no questions."

Judge: "At this time, the jury will be dismissed to deliberate. All members will be contacted when the jury has come to their decision. At that point we will reconvene here at the court house and read the verdict."

The jury was excused; everyone left the court house not positive on the outcome. The jury debated over a duration of approximately 3 days undecided on the verdict. There was no possibility for a hung jury due to the severity of the case as well as the amount of jurors. Finally, after much deliberation a decision was made. They sent a note to court to indicate they have come to an agreement on the verdict.

December4th, 1952 the verdict was in hand. The court clerk received the verdict from the foreman of the jury, read the verdict and passed it to the judge for approval. Judge Judy Patterson read the verdict and then passed the note back to the foreman to read it aloud. Jeff appeared to be nervous once again. Palms sweating, hands shaking and the thought of not seeing freedom filled him to the point of tears forming in his eyes.

Judge: "The defendant please rise and accept the judgement of this verdict passed to him by his peers."

Foreman: "We the jury find the defendant guilty on the first count of manslaughter in the case of Wayne Cartwright. We the jury find the defendant guilty of manslaughter in the case of Joan Cartwright and we the jury find the defendant guilty of manslaughter in the case of Dorothy Cartwright."

The verdict was handed to the judge once again.

Judge: "I personally thank the jury for all the patience and time spent in this case. Jury, you may have a seat." Jeff Thorton, your actions on the night of October 31, 1952 were criminal using alcohol and driving. There were three lives lost. Once again I thank the jury for coming to the right conclusion. Jury, you are here now dismissed by this court. We thank you again. Bailiff, please take the prisoner to holding. . The sentence will be delivered tomorrow at 10am."

The tears began to run down Jeff's face as he was taken away to holding by the authorities. All Jeff's family began to cry, they weren't even able to say good-bye. His mother began to sob and yell, "My Boy. My Boy." Bob immediately grabbed his mother to keep her from falling. Her legs began to give out as Jeff became further and further away from her arms. All attendees stood and exited the courthouse however the remaining were Jeff's family sitting in disbelief and tears.

December5th, 1952. As the courthouse was full of all who attended the trial, and more, there was no place to even stand. People were spilling out of the courtroom and into the hallways. Media were waiting with pad and paper in hand. This was the biggest story in 50 years, every newspaper wanted to be the first to print the news of his sentencing.

Judge: "Jeff Thorton of the township of Hillier, you are hereby sentenced to 10 years at the Kingston Maximum Security Prison with the possibility of early parole pending good behavior following a duration of 7 to 8 years. Take the prisoner away. Court is adjourned."

The judge slammed the gavel, stood up in her robe and left the courtroom. Jeff was taken to Kingston Penitentiary the same day. Bob collected his distraught family and piled them into the car. Bob's mother not saying a word. She had been up for the entire night crying. On the way home to drop off his parents Bob expressed he would guarantee he would get Jeff out of jail sooner than the time period he would have to serve before parole. To make matters worse due to the stress of the trial and having his youngest brother in jail Bob, Jeff and Julia's father passed away in the middle of the night right before Christmas. Funeral arrangements were made by his wife and son Bob. The entire family attended his funeral including Jeff. Jeff was granted a day pass to attend the funeral with high security measures taken by the prison of course. During the funeral Bob asked Julia, "Can you look after mom?" Julia responded, "You know I will. You must realize that she is pretty frail." Bob understood, "Yes I know, I hope she can cope with all this." "I hope so too." Julia said quietly. Jeff was taken shortly after the funeral came to an end. He was escorted back to Kingston Penitentiary by security. It was hard for his family to see him in chains and watched like a hawk during the proceedings. As Jeff was put in the van Bob stole a few moments to whisper to his brother, "I am going to come see you soon buddy. Next week. I have something to tell you." As the van drove away the tears and determination came to Jeff's eyes.

Bob went home with his wife however more arguments ensued so in result, no more sex, poor Bob. Bob was hiding the fact that he had a plan, a plan to get his brother out of jail. Those two brothers were really close, being twins. In the meantime Julia was looking after their mom. But mom did not look good in the days that passed, dad was gone and it was as though she had given up. There was not much for any of the family to do. She was looking more frail as the days continued, she refused to eat, really she had no appetite. She was wasting away right in front of them.

THE PLAN

Bob was a mechanic by trade so he started to devise a plan to build an airplane in the old barn at the back of his farm. He would go out for hours looking for parts and a kit to build a light plane. He determined it would cost him around $1500 for the kit. Katie nowadays seemed to not pay much attention to him. There was no more spark in their marriage; the light had begun to disappear as he searched for anything to build his plan. Once the kit was purchased he decided to go visit Jeff and divulge his secrets. Bob boarded the bus that took all visitors of the inmates to Kingston Penitentiary. The bus left at 8am and 12 noon every Thursday. When Bob boarded the bus there were people that looked as though they were going to a funeral. They appeared to be sad, upset they were going to see their loved ones, their family and friends. Bob was on the other side of the spectrum. He was happy, excited, and nervous to see Jeff. The entire way to the jail he felt as though he had not seen his brother in years, really it has been 9 months. Even though the bus had garbage on the floor, bars on the windows and ripped fake leather seats, he did not care. The ride was long and boring. The only thing that went through his mind was, "Observe. What is around me? How is this going to work? I am going to have to visit Jeff weekly to map out the area and where the guards are, who is watching and how Jeff is going to get where I need him to be and when." Once at the jail Bob arrived at the gate, it was huge. There were multiple fences that the visitors had to go through with keys and locks. As Bob stood waiting to be escorted by the guards through the multiple check points he looked toward the sky. All he could see was approximately 15 feet high with barbwire on the top. As Bob heard the buzzing to allow the guard to open the first check point he noticed one guard sitting in a chair up on a tower with his feet up on the ledge and a shot gun in hand. The guard at the gate had in his holster a regular hand gun. As the visitors passed through the multiple check points Bob took mental note of his challenges, AKA the armed guards. Finally 20 minutes after arriving at the jail Bob found himself taken through a maze of concrete to the visiting room. Bob was asked to spread his legs and hold out his arms. A guard patted him down to ensure he was not going to pass the prisoner anything; they were looking for weapons, goods, drugs. Jeff was escorted into the room where they had tables and chairs only separated by space and a glass plate window. As they took the cuffs off of Jeff both the brothers hands reached out for the glass as though they were going to be able to touch. Bob and Jeff sat in their designated seats and picked up the phone to their right.

Bob: "Brother, how you keeping up in here?"

Jeff: "Best to be expected. Really it's like hell. I sleep on a bed that is made of pure wood, they won't even give me a mattress, it's awful hard on the back, the food is trash, what do you expect I am a prisoner. "

Bob: "Don't say anything!" he said with a whisper.

Bob: "I have a plan."

Jeff: "A plan for what?"

Bob: "To get you out of here."

Jeff: "Are you insane? How do you intend to get me out of here? Don't do anything. You need to stay out there and taking care of the family. Correction services just informed me that I may be transferred to Joyceville in about a month or so due to good behavior. Bob, I am told that Joyceville is minimum security and it is a short distance from here. It is on highway 15 just north of Kingston. It is like a farm, no walls or fences."

Bob: "That's great! Even better. I have everything under control. I will let you know later how I will get you out. Just have patience and everything should be ready in about two months. Just don't get into any trouble in the meantime."

Jeff: "Are you sure? Because this is killing me being in here."

Bob: "Don't worry, I told you before I keep my promises."

There was this loud terrible horn over the PA. Time's up. The brothers said their good-byes and Bob made his way back to the bus but not before watching Jeff shackled and escorted back to his cell. It was about an hour and a half back to the county of Hillier and town of Consecon. Bob stepped off the bus and guess who was standing on the sidewalk? Lindsay just happened to be standing at the bus stop next to the drugstore.

Lindsay: "Hey Bob. How have you been baby?"

Bob: "What are you doing here?"

Lindsay: "Just a pure coincidence, I was going to pick up something at the drugstore."

Bob was very preoccupied with the situation in Kingston with his brother, however, not too preoccupied with the way Lindsay looked that night. She was dressed from head to toe in white; she blended into the snow like an angel. Her soft voice invited him into a further conversation. As they drew closer her hand reached out to his arm. They began to embrace which ended in a kiss. Bob's adrenalin began to rise. The one touch turned into an invitation to a drink to keep warm. They made their way down to the local pub. As they sat at the pub Lindsay inquired about Jeff and what was going to happen. They spoke for a bit about the hearing, the outcome and finally the funeral. By the end of the conversation Bob became more relaxed, he let loose, he began to listen to the quick wit remarks coming out of Lindsay's mouth as he closely watched her lips move. Bob began to have a good time and only thought of that moment, there was no thought about Katie his wife or his future plans. Lindsay's hand reached out to Bob's. Bob quickly suggested they leave separately and go to the hotel just down the way. It would be smart to leave separately. As they finished their beer, Bob got up and left, heading to the hotel to rent a room for the night. Before he left the table he instructed Lindsay to go to the concierge and ask for Bob Thorton's room. He would leave instructions to give her a key and let herself in. Approximately 20 minutes later Lindsay arrived at the room. She stopped before she entered the door to take a deep breath. Thoughts of being with him again rushed through her body and made her tingle from head to toe. She craved his kiss, she felt his touch every time she was home touching herself, masturbating. She exhaled and let herself in the door. Bob was lying on the bed dressed only in boxers. There was a couple drinks sitting on the table in the corner and a little Frank Sinatra in the background. Lindsay, being her kinky self, ran to the bed, jumped onto Bob.

Lindsay: "Tonight we are going to do this differently."

Bob: "What do you mean?"

Lindsay: "I want you to fuck me between the tits. I want your big balls rubbing my tummy. I am going to hold my tits around your cock and every time you come close to my mouth I will kiss your cock."

The dirty talk continued for a while as their blood began to race. Lindsay pushed him over, got on all fours and said, "I want you to ram me." He grabbed her hips and trusteed inside her. Wet, smooth, tight! He moaned with each thrust. His right hand move up to her right shoulder pulling her into him with every push. Leverage made every movement count. They felt every muscle in their body contract and release. Lindsay's back arched, her head came back toward Bob, his next instinct was to grab her hair. Lindsay screamed with pleasure as they then tumbled in the bed. Arms, blankets and legs rolled around as Bob caressed her body. She climbed on top of him as he sat on the edge of the bed. Her legs wrapped around him and pulled him deeper into her. His hands now both on the top of her shoulders as she moved her hips forward and back, up and down. How could a women move like that? Bob thought. His wife never moved like this. They pulled each other closer with every movement. They were getting closer and closer to climax. Finally they reached the climax together. Bob had not felt that kind of climax since the last time they were together, sweet release. They both lay on the bed laughing and smiling. After only a couple minutes Bob's mind was somewhere else. "Where are you?" Lindsay asked. Bob replied, "I am here sexy." He lied because all he could now think of is what he had to do for Jeff, what he was going to do for Jeff. Bob quickly rolled out of the bed and began to dress. He said, "I should probably go home, you are more than welcome to stay the rest of the night in the hotel room if you wish. It is paid for until tomorrow." Lindsay understood his situation and expressed her interest more to come later down the road. As the door closed shut behind Bob, Lindsay curled up and grabbed the remote to see what was playing on the television, with her luck Playboy channel was on and she was able to continue her sexual fun.

Once Bob reached home he found his wife in bed, it was past 2am by this time. He thought he would say hello to her however there was no response. He thought that he would be able to get away without showering because she was already asleep, Katie would not be able to smell another woman scent on him. Bob crawled into bed and fell asleep. In the morning Katie woke up around 6:30 am and thought she would make her husband some breakfast and find out what happened in Kingston. Katie felt sorry for Bob because he was struggling with Jeff's situation. Bob rolled over to wake when he smelt the coffee brewing and the sausage cooking. He walked into the kitchen, walked up behind Katie and gave her a squeeze, a kiss on the cheek and a soft "Good morning." Katie smiled and replied, "I have breakfast for you on the table honey. Sit down and lets enjoy, it's almost ready." As they sat at the breakfast table in silence Katie asked, "How is Jeff? How was your visit?"

Bob: "Well, he is fine but it is not easy. He complained about not having a mattress, he is sleeping on a wood bed and his back is now sore. I told him to be patient and it should get better."

Katie: "They did not even give him a mattress?"

Bob: "All he has is a heavy bed sheet over wood. His pillows are hard and small, it can't be too comfortable, he is in jail, it's not the Rits."

Bob finished his breakfast and said, "I am going to go out back to the farm and see if the stock is ok. The horses and pigs need attention. I might be awhile; I need to relax my mind."

While out in the farm Bob thought as he stared out into the old barn, this might be a great place to assemble the plane. The barn was about 100 yards from the house with tress and bushed between and his wife never made her way out there. His wife never paid much attention to him. It was going to be perfect. Katie would never think he was doing something in the barn if he spent a great amount of time in there. Decision was made. That is what he was going to do; he was going to build the plane in the barn. Bob felt encouraged when he made this decision; his plan was starting to take form. Bob decided to go to Trenton and take about ten hours flying lessons ,just enough to get his plane in the air and also being able to land as well.

It took approximately 3 month to build the plane. When Bob was not able to work on the plane any longer he would take a trip out to the Kingston Penitentiary to visit Jeff and update him on his progress. Every time

Bob arrived in the waiting room he had more and more information to share with Jeff. The progress of the plane was exciting as well as the security observations he made while coming up to the jail. At the completion of the 3rd month Bob decided to fire up the plane to see how she ran. As Bob turned the switch on he heard a sweet purr. It ran like a dream. Bob was such a happy man and so proud of what he had accomplished, he was really going to pull this off. Instantly, he jumped into the car to go visit Jeff and update him on the "PLAN". Once Bob arrived and shared the plan, Jeff was a little skeptical. Jeff asked Bob, "Are you sure the plane will fly?" Bob insisted, "Not to worry, everything is going according to plan." When Bob made his way back home he decided it's time to test his airplane for a short flight. The following morning 7am Bob found himself in the barn, pushing out the plane into the field. Once in position Bob jumped into the plane, revved the engine, heard her purr, let her run for about 10 minutes to make sure all parts were working fine. He prayed to be out of ear shot of his wife. Bob then began to push the throttle forward, over the next 500 feet he felt every bump in the field, and his mind began to race as he did not know if the plane was going to stay in one piece. After hitting 60mph she was airborne. He screamed with excitement. He went up approximately 500 feet so he would not be detected by any instruments. He was in the air for approximately 30 minutes. When he landed he felt the freedom and excitement he felt when he first took off. He successfully pushed the plane back in the barn to storage. Fait Accompli!

PART II – THE PLAN

Bob headed back to the house telling his wife he wanted to go hunting for a week and was leaving immediately. Katie did not pay much attention or cared where he was going. She said good-bye; have a good time. Katie's attention was paid to a two year old little girl so she really did not care what he was up too. Bob jumped into his pickup truck and headed towards Ottawa. Once he arrived he started to look around for a bank that was out of the way, more secluded. After a couple hours of searching he found a bank located on River Street in the west end of the city. It was on its own, pretty well isolated from traffic and crowds, good for a diversion. Bob headed to the east end of the city and found another bank on Riverside road; he decided that was the location he would rob.

As the sun goes down he prepared himself by getting a motel room to rest. As he woke from his deep sleep the sun was up. It was early, he decided to go steak out the bank, determine when the manager arrived at the bank, was he going to be alone? Would he have security? He waited outside dressed in a black hat. He watched as the manager arrived by himself. Yes, this is going to be perfect. All Bob had to do now was waiting for a rainy day to satisfy his plan execution. In the meantime, Bob drove to Valdor Quebec. This was an old mining town. There he was able to source out and buy explosives he will need in the bank robbery. Once at Valdor he went to a little hardware store, purchased himself a couple small clocks, some wiring, timers and explosives to do a proper job. He told the fella he was removing tree stumps on his farm in hopes to sway the thoughts of the salesman from thinking he was up to something illegal or unusual. Bob was smart. He proceeded to give the manager a fake name and address so he could not be traced. He needed to think of everything, every move to protect himself and his brother. After his planning and observations Bob decided to head back to Picton area, the weather was not cooperating with him. The sun was shining and no clouds in sight, the weather man even indicated the sun was not going away for the days to come. After arriving home to the farm he told his wife the hunting was not going well, it was not very good. He told Katie he would go back in a couple weeks. As the days pushed forward Bob decided to go and visit Jeff in jail, it has been a while and every time Bob looked in the mirror he would think of him. During the visit Bob disclosed to Jeff, "everything is working out, it is looking good for the escape. When you are transferred to Joyceville I will be halfway done with the plan but I need a few more weeks." To Bob's surprise Jeff advised him that he would be transferred to Joyceville in a couple weeks. "Great! This is working out perfectly." Bob headed back to the farm, finding his 2 year old daughter and wife sitting on the porch. He sat with them, playing with his daughter day after day, continuous looking at the weather. It will change Bob thought to himself daily. "Soon, I know it will." It looked like rain in the next few days so he decided to drive to Kaladar at Hwy 41. He turned North on 41, he could see nice lakes on either side of him, they were deep, deep enough and long enough to land a plane in. He drove about 10 more miles and saw another little lake with many boats inhabiting it at the moment. There were cars and trucks parked at the base of the lake, this lake was going to be perfect. He could land here and all he needed to find was an area that he would be able to hide a boat. It needed to be tree covered. He parked the pickup and walked along the lakeside. He kept walking for about 20 minutes and then there it was. There was the perfect spot to dock a getaway boat. As there were many boat dealers in the area he began to talk to the locals. He inquired to a few people and they instructed him to go about 20 miles down the road and talk to Jake. He is known to have the best service in these parts. He found a 16 foot aluminum boat which would be light to carry. It was a 5 hp Evinrude. He stocked up with rope, but just enough to tie the boat up, a small tent and essential camping gear which included a knife, small gas lantern, canned goods, a cooking pot, fishing gear, two sleeping bags, shovel, small hand held axe, bottled water & rubber boots. He paid cash for all items and proceeded to load all into the back of his pickup. Bob then headed back to his hiding spot on the lake with the aluminum boat. He parked and backed up the boat into the make shift driveway into the bush ending at the side of the lake in amongst trees. In this spot Bob found he noticed there was an erosion of dirt and clay into the water. He lowered the boat into the divot and decline, began to chop down small branches of the trees around him and covering the boat entirely with brush. "I can't believe it worked! You could hardly tell there was a boat hiding underneath all this foliage. The sky began to turn; everything was in place so the timing was right. The clouds were coming in fast, there was no time to get back to Picton, he had to take advantage of the weather. He jumped into his pickup and began to drive to Ottawa. He was trying to put the petal to the metal, he had to beat the rain. As he pulled into Ottawa the rain began to come down. It did not look as though it was going to let up. News insisted the rain was going to stay for the next 2 to 3 days. "Perfect!" Bob yelled as he drove in his truck. Bob began to think about his next move. He needed to find a motel room. Not the one he stayed in the week before. He did not want to leave any suspicion or tracks. He found another motel, The Red Light Inn. He pulled up to the motel and paid cash for a room. "#5" the clerk passed him the key and Bob grabbed his hat from the truck cab. As he walked into the motel room #5 he noticed some stains on the floor. Were they blood? Bob did not even want to think about what has previously happened in this room, if only the walls could talk he thought. Bob realized that moment he would truly do anything for his brother Jeff. Clearly. He is going to stay in this "Cockroach infested place for at least one night." He left the door propped open to then go out into the rain and get all other items out of the truck to assemble the bombs. Explosives, timers and clocks, check, he hides under his jacket as he moves into the motel room, he looks left and right to see if anyone is watching him before he closes and locks the door with force. He cleared off the table that was located to the right side of the bed. He carefully placed down each of the items on the table. They were all categorized, laid out with precision. He kept telling himself he must be careful with each item. He has not worked too much with explosives and did not want to make anything go off. He even insisted moving the table away from the wall heater located in the room. He decided to go out to grab a bite to eat before he came back to the motel to assemble the explosives. This would assist in not making any mistakes; probably a good idea. Before he leaves the room he places a "DO NOT DISTURB" sign on the door to ensure no one enters his room in his absence and finds the explosives and accessories sitting on the table ready for assembly. He sat down at the local dinner only ordering coffee and a poutine. He thought having a beer would be a bad idea, knowing what the late night events will include. As Bob enjoyed his Canadian poutine he remembered the times Jeff and him would go to the local dinner in town to enjoy a malt and poutine.

Bob makes his way back to the motel room, all up on coffee. He was going to be able to stay up and finish the explosives for the event tomorrow. He finds himself widely excited. His eyes are filled with a sense of accomplishment even before he has finished his task. He flings the motel room door open and finds the room just as he left it. A sigh of relief leaves his lips. He immediately sat down to begin to prepare the explosives. He gently picks up a couple sticks of dynamite and twines them together in a little package. He wired them up to the timer clock so when he set it, the clock would go off and ignite the dynamite. Next, he reaches into the bag and pulls out an old wool sock. He cuts out three holes, one for his mouth and two for his eyes. He makes his way into the bathroom, stands in front of the mirror, takes a deep breath, exhales slowly and pulls the sock over his head. As he positions the sock, holes over his eyes and mouth he smirks underneath. Finally he has done it. He can now get some sleep because he needs to be up by 5am to get in position. First he pulls out a flask of rye, he swigs down a good stiff shot. He lies down on the bed to try and go to sleep, nerves rush through his body. He can feel them everywhere. His mind is racing. Go to sleep. Go to sleep. He repeats in his head non-stop until finally his dreams grasp him and pull him in.

Bob wakes at 5am to the sound of rain hard against the window. "This is it! Perfect!" He jumps out of bed still in the same clothes from the day before. He compiled all his belongings and packed them into the cab of the truck. He climbed in and began to drive to the first bank on River Street. Bob parked his truck in a grocery store parking lot a half a block away from the bank. He looked around as he pulled into the parking spot. There was no one on the streets, no one in the parking lot. It appeared a little eerie. The rain caused most people to stay at home, he also considered it was very early in the morning, by this time it was about 5:30am. He began to walk to the rear of the bank placing his explosives in a space he found below cement steps, and covered the explosives with a small piece of tarp to ensure they did not get wet. If they did get wet there was a chance they would not ignite. He could not take any chance. Bob casually walked back to his pickup truck. He noticed there was still no one around. This could not be more perfect. He could not be seen placing the explosives. Bob got back on the road and headed to the second bank he found on Riverside Road on the other side of town. Since it was still early, around 6:15am, he was getting hungry. He stopped at a local restaurant "The Four Corners" ordered bacon and eggs, toast and coffee. As he finished enjoying his breakfast he noticed it was around 7:30am. He had enough time to park 3 blocks away from the bank, with him he brought the black sock, an old black coat, hat, a small amount of rope, a black duffle bag, black leather gloves and

Near Perfect Getaway

sunglasses. Being a mechanic it was not too difficult for him to steal a car, he walked up to an old 1945 Chevy, he casually let himself into the car and bent down in the seat pulled the wires down, cut two wires and crossed them. The car started right up. He did not peal out the parking spot, he casually drove off with full intention on returning the car after he completed his next task. Bob drove up to about 20 feet to the front of the bank, the rain was coming down so hard there was no one on the road, no one on the sidewalks. He put an old black coat on, the sock with holes on his head, a hat on top and sunglasses over the sock. There was no way someone would be able to identify him like this. Suddenly the manager of the bank is in plain sight. This is it! As the manager walks up to walkway leading up to the bank, Bob gets out of the stolen 1945 Chevy and walks in a timely fashion behind the manager. As the manager pushes the key into the door Bob is immediately behind him, pushes an old Colt 45 against the small of the bank managers back, little did the bank manager know the gun was not loaded. "This is a hold up! Walk into the bank, don't sound the alarm and just do as you are told if you know what's good for you." Suddenly, seconds before they entered the bank Bob hear sirens in the distance moving further away, he knew they were not coming after him, they were going to the diversion, the bomb had gone off at the first bank on River Street. All the policemen would be headed to that bank instead of coming here if anything went wrong in the bank robbery. Bob orders the manager to open the safe. The manager is still walking with the gun pressed up against his back in front of Bob. As they walk toward the safe the bank manager says, "You're never going to get away with this." As they approach the safe the bank manager begins to work the combination lock. His hands are shaking. He keeps repeating, "I have two small children. Please do not hurt me." The door clicks and the manager wheels around the lever to open the door. It is a large door, steal, heavy. Bob hands the duffle bag to the manager and pushes him with force on the gun into the safe. As Bob walks into the safe he sees an enormous amount of bills piled high on the shelves. His eyes widen with excitement and accomplishment. The bank manager tries to turn around to take a look at Bob. Bob's attention quickly turns back to the bank manager, "Don't turn around, don't look at me or I will fuckin blow your head off." Now the gun is pressed hard against the bank manager's head. The bank manager continues to place the unmarked bills into the duffle bag. Out of the blue Bob insists the manager passes him a couple bundles of cash so he is able to check the bills to ensure they are unmarked. They are clean. Bob screams at

Near Perfect Getaway

the bank manager to move faster. Finally the bag was over flowing. Bob quickly zips up the bag and orders the bank manager to leave the safe and sit in a chair, "Don't look at me" Bob screams. He turns the chair facing away from him, still pointing the gun against the bank manager. The bank manager does as he is told and sits in the chair facing away from Bob. Bob grabs the manager's hands and ties them to the chair firmly. He them moves to his ankles and ties them to the chair firmly. He ties his chest to the chair by wrapping the remaining rope around the chair and the man. He finally blind folds him with a tie and says very politely, "Thank you for your cooperation, your children will not be fatherless." Bob swings the chair to face the back of the bank and casually strolls out of the bank twenty-five minutes after it all began. He climbs into the 1945 Chevy, pulls off the black sock and returns the car to the parking space he found it. He walks from the car and over to his truck placing the black hat, sunglasses and coat on top of the duffle bag. He throws the duffle bag into the cab of the truck, climbs in and drives off casually. Bob is still very calm at this point, he knows he is not in the clear yet. As he drives he begins to see other cars and people starting their day, not knowing what he has done. As he is driving down the side roads he sees a tree stump which someone has extracted from the ground and thrown in a ditch with surrounding broken branches. He has an idea. He will lift the tree stump into the back of his pickup with some of the surrounding broken branches so he will look as though he is hauling wood and doing work, not just robbed a bank. Further and further away Bob travels from the bank he just robbed. He knows by the time the cops realize the bomb at the first bank was a diversion he is 1.5 hours from the scene on his way back to his home, Consecon. While driving he is listening to the radio. A news flash interrupts the music playing. The newscaster has a serious tone, "There has been a bank robbery in the city of Ottawa. There has been an attempt at the River Street bank, an explosion at approximately 8:45am. No money was taken however the police believe it was a diversion for the bank robbery which occurred on Riverside Road on the east side of town. No one was injured however an undisclosed amount of money was stolen." Bob begins to laugh because he has gotten away with the robbery. All this money! I wonder how much it is. He thinks to himself. He reaches the safe space of his county. No one will suspect him here. The radio continued to indicate they were searching within the city for a suspect. They would never suspect pulling someone over with his truck so far away. He drives to the backside of the farm which gave him access to the back of the barn. By parking here his wife would know he was home. When arriving he had to take a leak so bad he grabbed his flask, urinated in one area and then sat down to enjoy and celebrate his accomplishment, several big swigs of rye. After a little celebratory drink he takes the duffle bag into the barn, opens it and wants to count it. He decides to wait because his wife is known to walk out to the barn and just appear out of nowhere. He zipped up the duffle bag and took it out to the old outhouse which has not been used in years however it stilled smelled of shit. He dropped the duffle bag into the outhouse he then proceeded to place dry leaves, old newspaper and the branches he loaded into the back of his truck earlier that day on top to hide the evidence of his premeditated plan. No one was going to look there.

Bob walked back to the house and greeted his wife; he was in a great mood. He came in telling her that he did not have any luck hunting, he may try in a couple weeks. He thought he should be nice to his wife to ensure she would not go snooping. He needs everything to remain normal to ensure there is no heat from the police. Perhaps he might even get laid. Here's hoping. As he walked through the door she was very receptive to his arrival. She walked up to him and gave him a sweet salutary kiss. She led him to the bedroom with no words, just a slight gaze behind her into his dark green eyes. They began to dance around the room, slowly kissing. It was clear they have not touched each other in a while, there was hesitation in every movement. He grabbed her with both of his hands on either sides of her head. Her body suddenly melting in his hands. He instantly knew she was his to do whatever he pleased. He turned her around so her back and behind pressed against him, still moving their hips in a slow sensual dance. She moved her head to one side slightly looking behind her at him. He kissed her neck several times with butterfly kisses. It felt so good, so familiar. His lips slowly moved across her shoulders and down her right arm, he spun her around one more time to face him as he slowly grabbed her purple dress hem landing just above the knee. With one fluid movement he pulled her dress over her head so she stood naked. In Bob's mind he was wanting to try something new. He asked if she lay on the bed and wait just a moment. Bob ran as quick as he could out of the room to find something in the house to bring into the bedroom. Frantically looking all he could find was her knitting needles and thread. He quickly grabbed the thread and decided that this might be fun. He slowly strutted into the bedroom with a slight smirk holding the knitting thread behind his back. He looked at his wife and asked, "Do you feel adventurous?" She replied, "Whatever do you mean?" He slowly pulled out the knitting thread. Her eyes widened with excitement. They have never been adventurous in the bedroom before. He walked up to the bed and asked her to stand at the end of the bed facing the headboard. She did as he requested with no questions asked. He grabbed one hand and pulled it above her head, kissing the nape of her neck. He then proceeded to take the other hand and lead it up to meet the other. She was standing with both wrists grasped by one of his hands. He began to wrap the knitting thread around her wrists until she was fully restrained. Once he tied the knot he cut off the bundle of knitting thread he spun her around. He unzipped his pants and they fell to the ground. He pushed her down onto the bed with her hands over her head. He told her to grab the iron rod headboard pole and not to let go. He then leaned down to kiss her right above her right hip bone. She groaned as if she had never been touch before. He smiled enjoying her being vocal. He does not remember the first time he ever heard her make a sound during sexual contact in the past. He continued to feel her body and kissing her softly. More groaning. This is turning out to be fun! Suddenly he was inside her with a powerful force. She was fully aroused and enjoying him moving in and out. He progressively increased the force of the pounding and speed. Her body felt as it had never done before, she could not move her arms, her hands, she was bound in one specific position. Goosebumps she felt over her body and her hips flexed as she climaxed. Bob shortly finished following her lead. They lay silent as they have never been able to cum at practically the same time before. Following the silence Katie fell asleep. Bob kept thinking about the clothes from the robbery he forgot to burn. Thinking in his sleepy mind, "I will get up early and burn the clothes, get rid of the evidence."

The next morning he woke early 6am to get going on burning the evidence. He jumped out of bed not realizing his wife was not beside him. He walked into the kitchen to find his wife making breakfast and listening to the radio, not uncommon in her routine. He sits waiting for his breakfast and asks how she slept. She shushed him immediately, there was news breaking on the radio. The newscaster said, "It is officially a hoax! There was a bank robbery at one bank and an explosion at another across the city yesterday. Sargent Dan Comeau was assigned the case and leads the investigation reporting customers found the bank manager tied up at the Riverside Bank, there was a car found not too far from the bank that was assume to be a part of the robbery, a local man walked out to his car which was lock the night before and the wires were crossed. The car was finger printed and at this time there are no prints found other than the owners. The manager's description of the bank robber was that he had a black mask over his face, gloves and a black coat. There is no real evidence. The police are trying at this time to compare the robbery yesterday to previous crimes." Bob sat at the breakfast table tense. He knew after hearing the news report the police had no leads and he was going to get away with this, scot free. Finishing his breakfast he jumps up from the table not even waiting for his wife to finish. The excitement of getting away with this and knowing how much money was sitting in his shitter made him giddy. He grabbed his clothes from the robbery, the overcoat, the sock, glasses, gloves and a few small branches he threw in a pile on the ground far from the back of the barn so his wife would not know what he was doing. He doused the pile in gasoline and lit a match. Flames began to rise as a smile came across his face. After approximately a half an hour he put out the fire with dirt from the earth and racked up the pile so no one would suspect his actions. He ran into the house and said very somber, as the glee is jumping up and down inside him, "Honey, I think I should go see Jeff today. Would I be able to used your car to go to the jail? My truck is covered in mud and you know how I hate to drive a muddy car." She nods in approval and Bob grabs the keys just like a little teenager taking the car for the first time after he receives his license. Kingston bound Bob goes. As the jail courtyard becomes closer and closer Bob begins to literally jump for joy. He is beaming inside to tell Jeff all about the events that have occurred over the past couple days. As Bob arrives at the gates he is greeted by a guard dressed head to toe in combat armor, guns hanging off of him everywhere. Bob announces with pride that he is here to see his brother Jeff Thorton. The guard was very versed on the occurrences that happen at the jail on his shifts and he was working yesterday. The guard says to Bob, "Sorry, that prisoner was transferred to Joyceville yesterday." Bob's mouth dropped to the ground, visually distracting to the guard. "Are you not happy he has been transferred? No more barb wire or long enclosed tunnels to walk or drive through." Bob quickly recovered and said, "Of course I am happy, just did not expect for the transfer to happen without my knowledge, it is my brother." The guard politely asked Bob, "Do you know where the Joyceville Penitentiary is located?" Bob decided to play dumb. "No Sir, I don't. Can you give me directions? How far is it from here?" The guard gave him directions with haste. Bob backed up and continued on the road. Bob made his way to highway 15 toward Smithfalls, 10 minutes it would take to get there. This jail was so much different, no barb wire, he just parked in the parking lot and made his way into the penitentiary to ask for his brother at the reception desk, he politely spoke with the lady, a black hefty woman, sitting behind a glassed in area. "I am here to see Jeff Thorton, please?" The woman stood not saying a word. An eerie feeling passed through Bob as he waited for the gate to open. The women gazed into his eyes, never breaking the contact. The gate buzzed and the woman slowly opened the gate. As Bob walked through the gate with apprehensive movement he suddenly heard the women spout from her lips, "Spread dem!" The woman pushed Bob against the wall, his hands hitting the cold cement with force. She quickly spread his legs apart and began to pat him from under his arms down around his ankles. Bob was surprised at the event and tensed as she felt every crevice. When the women did not find any concealed weapons she back off slowly, between her clenched teeth she muttered, "Your lucky." She turned on her heels into the office he found her initially as he walked into the jail. She paged over the PA, "Jeff Thorton! Please come to the lobby! Jeff Thorton!" Jeff came down the hallway, strolling. He looked so different from the last time Bob saw him. He was dressed in a uniform, instead of bright blinding orange he was dressed head to toe in baby blue. A much more calming color if you ask me. As he approached, smiles on both of their faces appeared. Jeff held out his arms as though he was waiting for a hug. Bob hesitated because they were not even able to touch at the other jail. Jeff grabbed Bob in a loving embrace. "You found me brother! I knew it was not going to take you long." Jeff chuckled and Bob began to relax. "Jeff, are you able to take a walk?" "I can take a walk in the courtyard. There is no one out there." Jeff turns to the women which just moments ago accosted his brother Bob. "Can I take my brother Bob out for a walk in the courtyard?" The women responded with only a nod. Jeff led Bob to the courtyard. It was green lush grass with a weight machine in one corner and a baseball diamond in another. Bob was surprised of the "luxuries" there was for the prisoners. "Wow! This must be a cake walk in compare to the other penitentiary?" Jeff chuckled and nodded his head in the direction of Bob. "Let's walk toward the front gates." Bob said. As they strolled along they exchanged pleasantries as well as stories of the family back home. As they began to get further and further away from the courtyard door Bob said with excitement, "I have something to tell you brother." Jeff was surprised at his tone, stopped dead in his tracks to intently listen.

"See there across the road?" He pointed out into the distance over the road beyond the retaining wall, its only about 4 feet high.

"This is where I am going to pick you up brother. We have to set a time and a date. I have done everything. I have checked the weather for the next couple weeks. Let's plan for next Tuesday evening. It's going to take me approximately an hour. So, just at dusk. 9pm! You are going to see a little plane coming up over the horizon. Just be ready. Walk across the road and you will see me coming down with the plane."

"What do you mean plane? What are you talking about Bob?" Jeff said instantly.

Bob began to laugh, "I have not told you yet. I have a nice little plane that I have built in my barn. So, you will see me coming in from the south side. Once you see me run towards the plane, I will land quickly and you will have to jump in and then we will have to take off again and get the hell out of here." Jeff had this very confused look on his face.

"What the hell are you talking about?" "Just what I said. You just make sure you run as fast as you can and jump quickly in the plane and then we are gone. I will explain to you later about my beautiful plan. Just be on time. 9pm! You got it?"

"Got it! You are insane Bob! Do you have any idea what you are doing?"

"Yes! I know exactly what I have been doing. It has been in the works for a long time. GO! Get back inside. I will see you next Tuesday brother."

Jeff and Bob did not say anymore to each other at this point in time. They just walked away from each other, starring.

Jeff crawled back into his cell and lay down on the bed with a long sigh. He looked up at the ceiling with the biggest smile he has ever had before, from cheek to cheek. He instantly knew what has been happening in his brothers mind over the past couple months. He could not believe his brother cared about him so much that he would potentially risk his life, his marriage, his well-being, freedom, for him. During this time Bob was on the road, making his way home. He sang for miles. As he arrived home he found the house empty with a note on the kitchen table. His wife was gone to Picton for the rest of the day. "Thank you Lord!" Bob took a quick run out to the barn to ensure his wife had not been snooping. He fed the animals and decided he deserved a rest. He plopped himself down on the couch to watch a little television. Suddenly, she is home. The car pulled into the yard. His wife was home and he was no longer going to enjoy his rest. She too was surprised he was home. "How is Jeff doing honey?"

"He is doing well, he looks better and happy he is at a minimum security prison like Joyceville."

As the night moved forward they decided to go to bed, it was going to be an early rise so no playing between the sheets.

As the days pass, Bob tries to live normally without giving away his near future plans. As Tuesday approaches he ensures the plane is ready to go, the run way to take off is clear and the money was properly hidden in the outhouse and then moved to the back of the plane. Throughout the days as they passed he kept hearing a large tanker truck go by at the same time every day at 6:30pm. It was so loud it seemed as though it made the sand beneath his shoes move. He thought that this would be the perfect cover up to take off, his wife would never know. Tuesday night has finally come. The sun is shinning and birds are singing. Bob hardly slept Monday night in anticipation of the days to come. Bob shot out of bed like he had never done before in his life. Breakfast as usual with his wife in the kitchen. He was fueling not only for the remainder of the day however for the sparse days to come. "I have to go work in the barn honey!" He called out to his wife. This was not uncommon as she just continued to wash the dishes in the kitchen sink. Bob appeared to move as a 10 year old on Christmas morning. He bounced around the barn the entire day, ensuring all was going to go off with a hitch. 6:30pm. He opened the doors to the barn and rolled the plane out to the field. "It's time!"

He climbed into the cockpit and waited to hear the large tanker truck he heard every day around the same time. The earth began to move and he started the engine. The propeller started to turn round and round until he was ready to begin to pull forward. He checked all the instruments and started to lower the throttle. He saw the ground move beneath the plane, faster and faster he felt the plane go until finally it began to lift off the ground. His plan was to take a little time to fly around and sight see. It was not odd for small planes to fly around for a while and see the sights. He kept below 2000 feet to ensure he was not going to be on anyone's radar. At 8:55pm he rounded around near Joyceville. The time was here. "Here we go!" Bob said aloud. He began his decent toward the field. As he began his decent he looked to his left and saw a man running across the highway. He said to himself, "That's him! It's has to be him!" Jeff was running in the right area he needed him to be. Bob landed softly coming to a slow stop right on time. Jeff jumped into the plane in silence. Buckled himself in and they turned within the field to take off again. The speed began to pick up, faster and faster until they were able to take off. As soon as all wheels were off the ground they both looked around on the ground in silence still looking for security guards running after the plane but there was no one. The brothers yelled in glee as they reached 2000 feet in the air. "YAYAY! We did it!" Jeff immediately turned to Bob and said, "What the FUCK are you doing?"

Bob laughed with glee and said, "Saving your ass little brother!"

They banked to the left quickly and headed towards west bound 401. They set a course using visual rules. Bob had to look for power lines and highways to identify where he was in the sky. Thirty minutes into the flight Bob saw highway 7 and decided it would be best to follow. They adjusted their course and set out to stay on that heading for approximately an hour. This was going to give the boys some time to share some stories of the past couple months.

"Jeff, reach back and look in the duffle bag behind your by seat, it's covered by the blanket."

Jeff reached around the seat with his left hand and felt a bag. It was bigger than he expected. He turned his body right around and grabbed it with two hands pulling it onto his lap in the front seat. He looked at the bag and then Bob. With a large grin from ear to ear, Bob said, "Open it. I dare you." Jeff slowly began to unzip the bag, looking at the bag then at Bob and back at the bag.

"Holly Shit! Where did you get all this?" As Jeff grabbed the wads of cash from the bag. It was over a half a million dollars of crisp bills in the duffle bag.

"I robbed a bank in Ottawa." Bob laughed as the sentence passed through his lips. This was the first time he had told anyone of what he had done. He continued to tell Jeff all about the events and planning that went into the bank robbery.

"Let me tell you all about the events that have occurred since you were put in the slammer, little brother."

Jeff did not make a sound as he was stunned.

"So this is what I did. As I was sitting in court I thought of what could happen. What the worst scenario would be. And it actually happened. When I told you that I would get you out I meant it. So, I thought about first what we would need to live if I actually pulled all this off. I figured we needed money. I knew you did not have much and either did I so I decided to rob the bank. After thinking of all the movies we have seen on bank robberies, what the characters always did wrong was rob the bank and police would be right there for capture. I took my time to stake out multiple different banks in Ottawa. I figured being further away from home would be the best bet. I found a bank on one side of town and planted a homemade bomb under the back steps of that bank. This would draw the attention of police in the city. I made the bombs in a small hourly rented hotel room under a fake name. I watched the weather for days and decided it would be best to rob the other bank in the rain. There would be less people on the streets because I was planning on doing this first thing in the morning. I also watched the other bank for days, timed the arrival of all employees and their moves. It made most sense to approach the bank manager as he walked up to the bank. If it was raining there would be less people around. I would be able to force him into the bank and have him pack up the money, tie him up and still have much time before the other employees walked up. I timed it all perfectly. As I made my way to the second bank I decided it would be best to park my truck away from the scene just in case people saw me during the getaway. I jumped a car, a 1945 Chevy and drove up to the bank. I parked out front waiting for the manager and like the days I previously watched he arrived right on time. I was careful not to expose my identity as I walked behind him in the rain and held an empty pistol to the small of his back. I forced him into the bank, had him pack in the duffle bag all the cash. You should have seen it all stacked neatly, not knowing it was going to be soon in my possession. He begged for his life because he had children."

With shock on his face Jeff immediately shouted, "You didn't kill him?"

"Of course not you ass! I tied him to a chair, using the knots you taught me when we were kids. There was going to be employees arriving soon enough. He was going to be fine. The best part was, as I came up behind him and pushed the gun into the small of his back, the bomb went off at the other bank. Instantly you could hear police sirens in the distance and I knew I was not going to be bothered."

"You're fucking amazing Bob! How did you figure this all by yourself without having me around? Remember, I am the bad guy."

"What do you think? I am fucking stupid? I am the older brother so naturally I am the smarter one. Do you want to hear the rest or not?"

The brothers banked the plane to the north.

"Jeff? Do you see that small body of water up ahead?"

"Yes, I think so."

"That's where we are headed. We only have a couple minutes more so I will tell you the rest of the story when I can. We are going to have to pay close attention because it is very important what we are going to do next. I am going to land the plane not too far from the small island in the middle of the lake. There are a few planes that are parked in the water around the lake. A little more north up the lake is where the provisions are. We need to make it there. After we come to almost a stop I want you to turn the plane facing south while I run to grab something."

"OK. Whatever you say."

The landing was not as smooth as Bob intended however they were successfully in the water. Bob jumped out of the pilot seat and into the water running for the shore. He ran up to where the boat was located all covered in brush. He grabbed the dynamite and timers he planted there days before and ran back to the plane just as Jeff got the plane turned around. He placed the bomb underneath the driver's seat, he set the plane to idle speed and set the alarm on the bomb.

"I know you don't have any ID so I will through mine in. Can't forget this!."

Bob took his birth certificate as well as a couple credit cards and threw it in the back end of the plane in hopes the flames would not destroy the documentation to the point no police would be able to identify who was in the plane. Before they ran to take cover Bob grabbed the duffle bag of money. They stood in the water watching the plane idle off into the distance; it took about 5 minutes for the plane to reach about 300 yards from the shore. Both brothers ran to take cover from the blast. Momentarily the plane went up in flames. It was the best sight Bob had seen in days, other than the duffle bag of cash of course. The boys jumped for joy and shook hands. "We are finally free!" they yelled into the night. "We have to be extra careful for the next few days. Not draw attention to ourselves. We don't want the police on our trail."

The blast and fire was going to draw attention so they took off immediately. The dusk was upon them, by the time someone realized it was a plane that exploded in the middle of the lake they were on their way north.

Bob knew the closest police station was in Kaladar, at least 20 miles away. They had time before the investigation was to begin. They hauled the aluminum boat into the water. Bob first checked they had all the equipment he purchased however quickly coming to the realization they were not going to be able to do anything about it if they did not have everything. They put the motor in place and started the engine. It was surprising quiet as they began their journey into the unknown. They drove the boat in a relaxed manner not to draw attention to themselves. It was nearly an hour later as they headed north up the lake. Bob realized the police should be at the scene by now.

Three policemen arrived at the lake not knowing what had happened other than debris drifting in the water, some on fire. The flashlights were unmistakable and surrounding neighbors from at least a mile radius began to arrive trying to inquire about the nights events. One person which was a local approached one of the policemen, lunging into the water.

"I saw it!"

"Excuse me Sir, you must get back on shore. There are objects in the water which might injure you."

"Listen to me. I saw it! It was a plane that exploded. "

"Well, that is a police investigation matter. Give me your name, number and address; I will contact you for a statement at a later time. This is police business and we have to cover all bases."

As the police investigated with the assistance of a search light they called for a search boat to the area, around 11pm they decided there was no sign of life. It was then too dark to continue the investigation and they would resume in the morning. The lead investigator instructed two officers to resume the investigation on land. They were to collect the gentleman which approached them earlier that allegedly saw a plane explode in the waters and take him to Kaladar to collect an official statement. His name was George Bishop, he was known as the menacing individual of the community. After running a background on George Bishop the police found he had prior charges harassment, public mischief, public intoxication and domestic assault. Needless to say, his statement would not deem to be creditable. George sat on one side of the desk in the police station as Sargent sat opposite. George appeared to be visibly intoxicated however firm in his statement. "I tried to tell the police officer earlier what I saw tonight before I started drinking and he dismisssssss-ed me. I will tell you now. Tonight I was looking at the beautiful scenery, minding my own business with my friend Jack. Do you know Jack?" George pulled out an old flask from his back pocket and said to the Sargent. "Meet Jack!" Needless to say, Sargent was not impressed as he waved his hand and lowered his head dismissing the offer. "As I was saying, I was sitting, looking at the scenery and having a drink when all of a sudden I saw this plane then a big fucking explosion!" His hands flew in the air, his expression wide matching his arm movements out to the side. He almost flew off his chair as his arms violently swung from his body. Sargent quickly followed George's statement by thanking him. "I think we have all we need from you at this time. My fellow officer will see you home safe." Sargent gestured to the officer standing in the corner of the room.

By this time, Bob and Jeff were ten to twelve miles up the river. Bob said to Jeff, "I have another surprise for you." Bob drove closer to the shore and docked the boat. Bob jumped out and grabbed everything out of the boat, tent equipment, riffle, fishing gear and of course the most important the duffle of money. Jeff was led up a hill and down the road, 41 hwy, about a quarter of a mile away from the boat.

"I hope it is still there." Bob said with a smile. "What is still there?" "I purchased an old pick-up truck so we had multiple forms of transportation. I parked it at an old gas station which seems to be abandoned." They walk for which seemed to last for hours. "There it is! I can't believe it is still here." It was now just an hour before the sun rise. They needed to catch a little shut eye. They grabbed out the camping gear and walked into the wooded area behind the old gas station. The police would not be looking for them on the roads at this time of morning. The police did not even have a clue to which form of transportation they were using so they could rest easy and prepare for the rest of their getaway. Bob and Jeff protected the most important item they carried with them. They slept with the duffle bag of money under their heads.

The sun was up and the tent was hot as hell. Satin was licking their toes. Bob and Jeff slowly opened the windows of the tent keeping an eye out for anyone in the surrounding area. If they saw someone they knew they would be able to explain a story that they were out four by fouring and got their vehicles caught up in a mud swamp, walked until they found road and had tent equipment by chance. Yes, that would be the story. Rest assured when they looked out the windows there was no one in sight. They both took a deep breath, looked at each other with a big sigh of relief. Quickly they broke down the tent and packed up all their belongings. Bob and Jeff immediately jumped into the pick-up. Bob driving of course, he was the one who knew where they were headed. Jeff turned on

Near Perfect Getaway

the radio in hopes to not hear a thing about the escape, the explosion and getaway. Following 10 minutes of driving the radio illuminated with a serious tone.

"In further news. Last night there was a plane which exploded on Mazinaw Lake. There were no bodies found however foul play is suspected. The police have been investigating throughout the night with little evidence or information indicating what did occur. Witnesses have only identified the blast and no suspects involved. We will keep you up to date on the occurrences as they are identified."

"YES! We did it! This is the best day ever!"

The boys celebrated in the cab of the truck. They could now put some distance between them and the plane blast with no worries. Halting the celebration abruptly Bob interjected. "OK. We need to come up with a plan in which we will tell people when they ask what we are doing or where we are headed." "I've got it! It's so simple. We are two brothers that are looking for an adventure while being surrounded by nature. Just look at what we are carrying. Fishing gear, tent equipment, hunting gun if you will. We will tell people we are just wondering for fun." "Great idea Jeff. So stick to the story."

As they headed north on highway 41 Jeff pulled out the map. Bob pulled the truck over to explain to his navigating partner where they were headed. Bob pointed to Lake Manzinaw and said "Here. This is where we are." His finger slowly continued up highway 41, west along highway 28, then to a cut off to highway 121 in Paudash straight west headed toward Huntsville. "We need to make our way towards French River." Jeff studied the map and analyzed how Bob came up with the route mapped out for them to follow as Bob pulled out onto the road. Until this point Jeff did not realize how much time, thought, money and consideration Bob put into this plan they were now following. Jeff felt lost in a black abyss of nothing however he knew then and there one person he could count on and follow into the unknown was his brother. Blood bonds cannot be broken. As time passed they found themselves coming up to Huntsville. They found a little country dinner called The North Star. They parked right in front of the dinner in order to keep an eye on their truck as they ate as well to appear they were acting normal and had nothing to hide. The boys walked in trying not to draw attention to themselves. That did not work as well as they hoped. They were from out of town and all in the dinner knew it. They had grown out facial hair and did not intend on shaving. They thought the hair growth would blend in better as well as conceal their identities in the northern areas. All heads turned and looked at the boys as the bell rang at the door. They did not stop as many would have by being stared at by a bunch of strangers. They continued to walk straight for an empty booth along the window. They grabbed menus as their hunger became more apparent. Jeff was practically salivating looking at the menu. You do have to realize he has not had regular food in quite a few months. Jail food was not very satisfying. Jeff looked at Bob flashed him a big smile and said, "I want one of everything brother." "Get what you want Jeff. Fill your belly. It may be a while until we stop again." The waitress looked older than sixty with a short brown and white serving dress and a pair of nursing shoes. Her eyes showed a hard struggle of life however she was trying to cover her years with bright blue eye shadow and fake eye lashes. "What can I get you boys?" Jeff popped in his seat, "I will have a coffee, water the largest Poutine you have and the Great Canadian Burger please." Bob chuckled, "I will have the same." "Coming up!" The waitress turned on her heals and placed the order with the kitchen. "You had to go all out and have everything you missed, didn't you Jeff?" Jeff smiled from ear to ear. He leaned closer into Bob and whispered, "Listen, they serve you shit in jail. Every day I had stew with no taste or just hunks of meat, potato and veg. Nothing had taste. We could not choose what we were going to have and let me tell you something

... you really miss the food you enjoyed on the outside." Jeff sat back in his seat, obviously relaxing, and returned his voice back to a normal level and tone. "So, on that note, I am going to indulge in the finer things in life. I am going to sit here and enjoy the crisp texture of fries with a softer interior, squeaky cheese curds melted by salty, tasty gravy. Following 'the stroke in a bowl' I am going to enjoy the Great Canadian Burger which will tantalize my taste buds with an all-beef burger topped with lettuce, tomato, onion, ketchup, mustard, mayo and a couple pieces of peameal bacon. UMMMMMMM!" Suddenly, the food arrived and it was everything and more of what Jeff just described. The boys sat in silence just devouring their lunch. As they finished they both sat back rubbing their bellies very satisfied. The cheque was placed on the table during their eating fest, they quickly paid the bill however right before they stood to their feet they heard the radio music cut out and a serious announcement interrupt.

"Attention! Following the investigation which involved a plane explosion occurring on Lake Manzinaw has discovered new evidence. A local fisherman has pulled from the waters a floating credit card marked with the name of Bob Thorton. Police intend to further investigate the new evidence. It has been discovered Bob's Thorton's brother Jeff Thorton has disappeared from Joyceville Minimum

Security Prison. It is assumed there is a connection. Witnesses have given statements to support the theory the Thorton Brothers landed in the lake with the plane in question. Stay tuned for further information. We will keep you updated to this bizarre incident." Bob and Jeff slowly continued to rise in their seats and make their way to the door and into their pick-up.

Police arrived at Bob's residence with the intention to speak with his wife Katie. As the police pulled into the long drive Katie came out of the house to politely welcome her guests. She has been listening to the radio and Bob has been gone for days now. She knew this had something to do with him. The police men exited the cruiser and slowly walked toward the house. Katie watched them walk in the country wind and finding the cops easy on the eyes. She thought to herself, *WOW! He is not bad looking!* "Good afternoon gentlemen. How can I help you?"

"Mrs Thorton, my name is Sargent Dan Morrison and in light of the recent events we would like to ask you a few questions about your husband. Is he home?"

"No officer. Bob has not been home for almost one week. He said he was going to go Moose hunting. Regularly when he is hunting he is gone for a couple weeks."

"Where does your husband usually hunt?"

"Up north, that's all I know. I have never really cared to inquire further."

"Do you mind ma'am if we take a look around your property?"

"Of course not officers. Please let me know if you need anything while you take a look around."

"Thank you."

The police men strolled around the houses exterior. Once they came to the back of the house they could see the old barn. They took their time walking toward it looking for any evidence which would give them a better idea of what occurred with Bob and his brother. As they got closer to the barn they noticed grass which appeared to be flattened by something. Upon further investigation they noticed tracks which spread about 300 ft. There were three tracks which could have been made by a private plane. The police discussed the take-off and imagined it was a rough one. As the police entered the barn they also noticed a large space which was bare now. Once there would have to be a large piece of machinery stored there. Beside the bare area they discovered multiple wooden crates, partially dismantled. Marked on the crates were black letters which indicated the address, RR#2. Upon further inspection the return address indicated the crates originally came from Wichita Kansas. The police took down the Kansas address in their note books and continued to inspect the space. A great magnitude of tools was within arms-reach. Assuming Bob did build a plane he had all the tools necessary to accomplish his task. In amongst the tools there were also parts of machines, possibly other planes. The police concluded their inspection and returned to the house to question Katie Thorton further.

"Mrs Thorton? Do you know what your husband did out in the barn?"

"No, I never went out to the old barn. We have a newer barn just down the meadow that Bob built approximately five years ago."

"Did he ever talk to you about any other activities he was involved in? Other than fishing? Hunting?"

"No. He was not a very talkative type of person."

"Mrs. Thorton, I would like to inform you that the police have found a credit card floating in Lake Manzinaw with your husband's name on it. I am sure you heard about the plane that exploded in Lake Manzinaw. Your husband's brother Jeff Thorton has escaped from prison and we believe there may be a connection. By observing the track marks outside as well as the contents of the barn, I am sure we can make a definite connection."

"What do you mean? You're not suggesting Bob broke Jeff out of jail?"

"That is exactly what I am suggesting. Do you remember hearing any excessive noise coming from the old barn area the day your husband left?"

"No. I hear lots of noise. There is a great amount of traffic that comes down the road. I hear anything from tractors to big trailers hauling livestock."

"I believe your husband built a small private plane in your barn without your knowledge and when he said he was going hunting I think he had full intentions and plans to break your brother in-law out of jail. I will put money on it."

"We will see you are wrong when he comes home in about a week or so."

"If you hear from him please give us a call. Do not leave town because we may have more questions for you. Thank you for your cooperation."

Katie's mind began to race as she entered the house closing the door behind her. She leaned up against the door, hardly able to stand. *Did he really leave me?* She slid down the door way, losing her footing beneath her. Her head in her hands and the tears began to flow.

Leaving the Huntsville area the boys continued on their journey heading North on Highway 11 toward

North Bay. The news broadcast which occurred at the North Star made them think they needed to be a little more careful. "Fuck. We have to get off the roads." They continued to drive for hours and hours on end, stopping as little as possible. Bob and Jeff began to talk about the plan ahead. They decided together to get off the roads as quickly as possible. Destination French River. They planned to find a boat dealer and purchase a cruiser. Jeff pulled out the map Bob had stashed in the glove compartment. Jeff followed Highway 11 all the way to Callander. As Jeff looked at the map he recalled Callander being a small town, about 200 people, Bay type area, with only a couple restaurants on the top of the hill. They will appear to be just two brothers out on an adventure together. It would be too risky to drive to the French River. This way, stopping in Callander, they would be able to start their aquatic journey at Lake Nipissing. If they were to follow Lake Nippissing West they would run into the French River and follow the lakes and rivers further west.

As they pulled up to Callander there was hardly anyone in sight. They drove alone the lakeshore in hopes of finding a boat dealership. They came across a small dealership called Callander Motors. Leaving the duffle bag locked in the truck both boys climbed out of the truck with a smile from ear to ear. A short plump gentleman greeted them warmly as they walked closer to the boat section of the yard. "Well hello there! You folks from out of town?" Bob extended his hand out to the gentleman and introduced himself as John from Wooler area. "What are you boys doing way up in these parts?" Bob took control of the conversation, "We are just two brothers looking to spread our legs out in the water. A little fishing would be just what the doctor ordered, if you know what I mean." All gentlemen began to chuckle in agreement. They began to walk around the shipyard and talking about the different watercrafts available. "What kind of boat you boys looking for?" "We are planning on going into some rough waters eventually so perhaps a twenty footer with sleeping quarters which sleeps two and can handle the kind of waters." "I have just the one!" The salesman walked them around the yard and stopped in front of the "Bay Liner! Come aboard gentleman." They climbed into the boat with ease. Smiles from ear to ear. As they continued to explore the many areas of the boat their heads continuously nodded. "This is it!" Bob proclaimed. "We will take it! I assume you take cash?" Surprisingly the salesman turned around in one swift movement and uncontrollably replied, "Yes of course!" As the deal came to a close the boys asked for a little privacy to collect the money. The salesman was very excited to close the deal and graciously accommodated their wishes. The door closed tightly behind the salesman, the boys could not but noticed the grin on the salesman's face as he closed the door, leaving his head being the last body part that left the room between the frame and door. They quickly collected and counted $6,000. After the $6,000 was removed from the duffle bag, Jeff looked at Bob and said, "Fuck! How much is in here?" "I have no idea. You are welcome to count it if you like. Let's get out on the water first." The boys walked out the office door and handed over the $6,000 in cash to the salesman. "We will hook up now if you don't mind. Can you also give us some directions to the nearest boat launch?" As Jeff and Bob began to hook up the boat to the truck the sales man wrote out directions. It was only about 10 minutes down the road.

While driving to the boat launch Bob instructed Jeff on how they were going to launch the boat and then ditch the trailer separate from the truck. "I think we need to destroy this truck Jeff. I think we should launch the boat, tie it up to the dock, park the trailer in the parking just off of the launch area and then take the truck and burn it. What do you think?" "Let's just ditch the truck, fuck burning it." "What about the evidence in this truck? People can find our fingerprints in it." "You have a point there. Where should we ditch and burn?" "Let's check out the launch, go to a store and grab some food to take on the boat then go for a drive and find a place. I am sure there are abandoned buildings where we can park and burn it. We will have to do it just before dark." As they pulled up to the boat launch there were empty docks, it was perfect. They decided to launch the boat immediately and leave it at the dock, they parked the trailer in the parking just near the launch. They decided to take care of the shopping and truck. As they drove around the small area of Callander they found an abandoned garage. Up the road about a mile they found a grocery store and gas station to purchase gas, food and small provisions which they will need on the water. They bought mostly canned goods and dried food so they did not have to cook as much. They did purchase some fresh food as well to accompany their fish they would catch out on the water. Tonight they will have steak and potatoes as a celebration dinner. Once they finished the shopping the sun was beginning to go down and it was time to torch the truck. They parked it behind the abandoned garage, doused it in gas purchased from the gas station, lit a match and they began to run like hell. As they ran through the woods they continuously looked behind to see the flames coming from the truck. When they reached the boat at the launch they hurled all bags aboard and unravelled the rope. The motor began with a sweet purr, off they went not looking back, however only hearing the fire truck sirens in the distance as they became further away from the shore. A half an hour of sailing later they turned on the radio. A few song later a news bulletin interrupted.

"On the news tonight! More on the plane explosion on Lake Manzinaw. To date there has not been any bodies found which could be tied to the event. It has been concluded possible subjects involved, Bob Thorton and Jeff Thorton. The investigation clue found was a floating credit card inscribed name of Bob Thorton in the waters as well as Jeff Thorton's escape from Joyceville prison. The subjects are not known to be alive or dead at this time. Anyone with information on these individuals are asked to call the police. Due to the increasing weather complications and ice forming on the lake, the investigation will be continued when the ice melts. At that time it is hoped the bodies will resurface and the investigation will be concluded. Police will continue to investigate the happenings of that night on solid ground."

Bob and Jeff were now in the open water away from the police trying to hunt them down. They began to get dinner ready and relax with a drink also purchased that afternoon. As long as they stayed out of the police boats radar they would have no issues in their journey. Dinner was nicely grilled to perfection steak with grilled asparagus and a baked potato. This was the most mouth-watering, fulfilling meal they have both had in a long while. As they sat back with a satisfying bottle of cold beer they smiled at each other knowing this was just the beginning of their journey. They had miles and miles to travel however they were together and were each other's protectors.

The brothers headed west toward the French River which was approximately 80 miles of open water from the point of launch in Callandar. As they travelled toward the French River they could feel the miles creep on their faces which slightly resembled a more than a 5 o'clock shadow. Feeling less than fresh they discussed docking at an island, Sandy Island, which was at the mouth of French River. There they would be able to assess where they were and where they were headed the following day. As they docked and became land bound they discussed a trim of their faces. While trimming their face hair they discussed an interesting topic. "Hey Jeff! I have heard you are able to change your name legally when you hit Winnipeg. I think this will be a great way to disguise our identity. What name would you pick? Who do you want to be?"

"Grant Smith! I have always wanted to be called Grant. I never really saw myself as a Jeff. What name would you choose?"

"I have never really thought about it. How about John Smith?"

"Really? That is such a plain name brother."

Bob began to laugh out loud, "I think it suits me. I think it is a plain name like Jane Doe. I am nothing like a John Smith or Jane Doe so I believe it will be mysterious to people that get to know me in the future."

"Do you think we should start to call each other these names now? So we get used to them of course."

"Good idea. Good-bye Jeff Thorton, hello Grant Smith!" Bob held out his hand to his little brother with a firm shake.

"Good-bye Bob Thorton, hello John Smith." They both smiled as they shook hands embracing the future to come. The beers continued to flow and they brought out the map to determine their route for the following day. It was just the two of them for as far as the eye could see. They followed the map west from Sandy Island where they were at this point in time to the opening of Georgian Bay. Bob told Jeff all about the stories he has heard in the past about the Indian reserves and settlements which reside all along the French River. This may be a great opportunity to bargain with them for more goods they may need in their travels. They thought about even buying gifts from the reserves to exchange for favors in Winnipeg. As the night continued to overcome the sky their heads found a soft surface to embrace them in sleep.

As the sun began to rise the brothers began to cook breakfast, bacon and eggs, toast and hash browns with a nice cup of coffee. Their breakfast was also known as the breakfast of champions which included beer and tomato juice. In their journey so far they have met a gentleman which told them there was an Indian Reserve, Huron Tribe, just 30 miles from Sandy Island. They could ask for the Chief, Powow Lee. He would be able to supply them with the goods needed and information of what was further down the river. As they approached Huron Tribe two hours later, they were greeted by signs indicating "Approaching Indian Reserve Little Creek." They approached with vigor and vitality in their step. As soon as the boat was docked they tied the ropes and took in the landscape in the distance. There stood a teepee on the horizon and there must be answers ahead. They began to take foot. As they approached the teepee they believed it was under the ownership of Chief Powow Lee. Suddenly Chief Powow Lee was in plain view. He exited his teepee to discover the travellers set in front of him. The brothers thought it would be respectful to continue to use their given names, Jeff and Bob, while in the presence of the Chief. Both brothers extended their hands in peace towards Chief Powow Lee explaining they travel from the USA to their great lands. After the brief introduction Chief Powow Lee speaks, "Come, Come, Your Welcome." Motioning the brothers to duck and enter the teepee. Bob and Jeff politely accepted the invitation even though they did not know what to expect. As they entered the teepee a vision of beauty sat before them. She had dark brown straight hair and beautiful olive skin with the eyes of a eagle. She was breathtaking. Chief Powow Lee continued without hesitation or observation of the brothers reaction to the young lady sitting cross legged on the floor. "My daughter, Princess." He gestured toward her. "She looks like her mother; she passed over about ten years ago, many moons. Princess takes care of me now. Her good woman." Both brothers jumped at the opportunity to greet her. The politeness of the brothers continued. They bowed and commented on the beauty of the Chiefs daughter. All four joined the circle cross legged, in respect of course. Both Bob and Jeff felt uncomfortable in this cross legged sit, it was very noticeable physically. They practically had to hold each other up from falling down. Princess found their behavior and respect comical; a slight giggle coming from the direction of Princess lifted their heads. Chief did not find her giggle acceptable and interrupted with, "Where you boys headed? Coming all the way from the USA you must be determined." Bob answered immediately because this is what he suspected the Chief would be interested in. "We are heading west and hope to get to Vancouver eventually. We are presently travelling by boat." "Well, with that kind of travelling ahead you must join us for dinner and perhaps camp out here." The brothers were very grateful and accepted immediately without hesitation.

A part of the Huron Tribe tradition it was customary the welcomed guests were to be pleased. Princess without hesitation jumped up from the cross legged position and ran out of the teepee. She began to build up a little fire in the stone pit and proceeded to take the meat hanging on the line, I believe it was Caribou, and place it over the fire rack. The look on her face was so exhilarating. Many more of the Indian residence joined them around the fire. Conversation around the fire was non-interrupted. The brothers seemed to mesh into the community without much effort given. Good thing to know because this reserve was well known for killing those in which they did not like, if you know what I mean. Princess was a vision to be enjoyed throughout the conversations with all the other Indian reserve residence. She was very pleasant and forthcoming with information of what we were going receive from the tribe. As soon as she came up to the brothers and let them know dinner would be in a few minutes she sat beside the brothers with no hesitation. Chief Powow Lee noticed his Princess was observing both the brothers and he realized she was ready. Her lips were moving with the words they both spoke and her eyes were seeing right through theirs during conversation.

Dinner was now served. It was the most uncivilized display of a meal that Bob and Jeff have ever experienced before; completely eye-opening. There was so much out there then either of them have ever experienced before. It was completely natural for this culture to just tear off a chunk of meat from a turning carcass over the fire and eat with their hands. Really it was heaven for Bob and Jeff. As the mouths chomped down on the meal, Chief Powow Lee pulled back from the meat and acknowledged, "Good." Princess was observed by both brothers chewing on the bone of the Caribou. Princess took the bowls of bones which were left from dinner and brought them to her dog.

As they completed the offerings the conversation continued. Smoking the peace pipe followed the commencement of eating, friendship was established; at that time Chief Powow Lee decided he would intervene in the conversation to move things along following dinner. The White man has come to inquire about their culture and enjoy their way of life. Chief was not blinded by this thought however, he came to the conclusion that perhaps the boys were running from something back at home. His little Princess was mesmerized by their presence and did not hide that fact. Princess asked the brothers, "Can I see your ship?" Jeff hopped up from around the fire and said, "I will show you the boat!" Bob did not even have the chance to get up or respond when Jeff and Princess were walking towards the boat. The stars lined the way to the boat. They walked and talked about her way of life on the reserve. When they reached the boat he took her hand and helped her onto the boat. Princess boarded the boat with grace. Jeff showed her around, first the top deck and then down below. She walked into the kitchen area and then into the bedroom where the boys would sleep. There she saw a duffle bag full of money and said, "Gift for me?" Jeff replied, "NO! However I can help you if you are nice to me. Would you do as I say?" "I will do anything you say for a gift I can give to the Chief." "Do you have your own place? Do you have your own teepee?" "Yes. Not far from my father." "Can you maybe later tonight get away and come visit me on the boat?" "Yes my father sleeps pretty well. I will give him . . . " "We have some good stuff here on the boat. Would your father like something like Whiskey?" "Yes he loves Whiskey!" As Jeff grabs the bottle of Whiskey, smile stretched across his face says, "Whiskey it is!" They walked hand in hand back to the tribe and party waiting. Jeff walked up to Chief Powow Lee and said, "Gift for you kind Chief!" Chief Powow Lee saw the bottle of Whiskey and said with excitement in his voice, "Me like, me like Whiskey!" The festivities continued through the night, passing the Whiskey bottle around and drinking the Whiskey right out of the bottle. As the bottle slowly decreased in Whiskey, Jeff and Bob noticed Chief Powow Lee begin to weave and sway back and forth. Bob and Jeff suggested they retire to bed and they insisted they help Chief Powow Lee back to his teepee as he sung his cultural tunes. Meanwhile, Princess did not have so much to drink so she was distracted with men on her mind. As the boys walked back to their boat Princess was not in sight. As the boys boarded the boat they pulled out a couple beers out of the small cooler and sat underneath the millions of stars. They continued to speak of the future and the past enjoying each other's company. Meanwhile, back at the reserve Princess was not sound asleep in her bed, she was actually thinking of all the adventure she could have if she did sneak out of her teepee and visit the mystery men on the boat. They seemed exciting and inviting to her. "I can't wait any longer" she said under her breath to herself. Princess immediately poked her head out of the teepee to see only a few people sitting around the fire still burning. They seem intoxicated; they will never even notice if I begin to walk toward the water, she thought to herself. In one foul swoop she shot out of her teepee and casually began to walk toward the water, inconspicuously. The thoughts of responses rushed through her head. "That's it, that's what I will say when they ask me where I am going. I will tell them I am going to dispose of waste and it is none of their business. That will shut them up so they don't think of me again." As she continued to walk, her walk became a brisk walk and then a run as she became further and further away from her tribe. She ran toward the small glowing amber of light coming from the boat. She all of a sudden stopped in her tracks, took a deep breath and continued to walk nonchalantly. As she approached she grabbed the rope to steady herself, careful to not embarrass herself. She slowly stepped onto the boat and made her appearance known. "Well hello Miss Princess!" The two brothers looked at each other with a devious smile. "Would you care for a drink?" Immediately she replied "Yes." She took the drink with a smile as they both tapped the seat between them. She sat down without hesitation. They began to talk about the tribe and how she lives on a day to day basis, eventually moving to the question, "do you have a boyfriend?" She smiled and said with a soft voice, one they have not heard come from her lips, "no". She reached out to Jeff's inner thigh and rested her small gentle lady hand upon him. Jeff leaned in to kiss her on the neck as she reached to put her drink on the small table close to her knees. That hand did not come close to her body as expected; she reached out for Bob's inner thigh as she sat back. Bob then leaned in to kiss her softly on the neck. This was becoming interesting. With no words all parties knew what was going to happen. Princess turned to Jeff, looking into his bright blue eyes, they were intoxicating. She leaned forward and kissed his soft lips. She then turned and leaned forward to kiss Bob, feeling the difference between the brothers. The heat began to warm in their veins. Princess began to feel a slight tingle between her legs, one she invited with a soft smile. What was not expected is that she became dominant, controlling of the men's movements. She turned back to Jeff and firmly grabbed his face, a hand on either side, and kissed him passionately. She kissed as though she had never been kissed before and only dreamed of the moment. As she slowly let go with one hand she reached behind her to pull Bob close, inviting him to join in. Bob grabbed her hair and pulled it to the side forcing her lips onto his, he wanted to kiss her more now than before. His wife had never took control while they kissed or had sex. This was exciting to both men. This was a woman that knew what she wanted and was going to take it. Bob pressed his chest upon her back while Jeff began to pull the ties of her tribal dress. As Jeff pulled only one small string the cloth dropped from her shoulder exposing her perfect breast, taught upright nipple. Her skin appeared to be flawless. Jeff kissed from her neck down to her breast, taking her nipple between his teeth. As he bit down she inhaled sharply throwing her hands above her head and back to Bob grabbing him to pull him closer. Bob pulled the other tie on her dress to expose her other nipple. Bob reached around and felt her young breast while kissing her back, making the blood flow. The men were hard as rocks and ready to take her on. Bob spread his legs to pull Princess up onto his manhood. Have her feel the strength he had between his legs. She moaned. Bob pulled her close and reached between her legs. She was wet. She was so turned on by only kisses and slight touch. Jeff pulled down his pants and knelt on the boat bench, erect and waiting for her mouth to engulf him. Princess reached out to him, feeling his shaft and licking her lips. Bob lifted up her skirt and placed her slowly onto his penis. She moaned again as Bob entered her wet lady bits. She leaned forward in pleasure and too Jeff into her mouth. Princess began to move her hips up and down, back and forth enjoying the length and girth of Bob, she also was enjoying the stroking of Jeff. Her eyes were smiling as she sucked, licked and cupped Jeff's balls. As they moved together the sounds became louder, more pronounced. Princess wanted to be shared so she rose up off of Bob to then turn around and bend over. As she lifted up Bob noticed a little blood. Startled to realize she must have been a virgin. Not saying anything Jeff grabbed her hips and slid inside her. Over and over again he forced her upon him. The sex with Jeff was rougher with Jeff then it was with Bob. Princess thought perhaps it was the position however Jeff felt deeper, made her feel more full. It felt better. As she continued to take Bob into her mouth he became close and closer to climax, he came into her mouth as Jeff came into her. Princess lifted her body she looked into Bob's eyes and said, "Wow! That tasted good. A little salty but good." They all laughed and relaxed together as she tied up her dress once again to be covered. Princess went to the bathroom to clean herself up then to come out to finish her drink and asked for another. Jeff jumped up immediately to succumb to request. The three continued to talk and drink not realizing the sun was about to come up. Jeff, true to his word, went to the duffle bag and pulled out the $5000 as promised. He handed it to Princess, without saying a word put her glass down and began to walk back to the reserve with the promise never to speak of the event again.

While walking back to the reserve Princess was excited. She had experienced sex for the first time and had fun doing it, in a little bit of pain and discomfort but she had fun. She also had the opportunity to bring home lots of bills which would help out her father and the rest of the tribe.

Princess made her way back to her tent to rest; it was about 4am so her eyes were heavy even though her mind was racing. As the sun rose her eyes opened wide still excited of the events from the previous night. She ran into her father's tent in hopes to find him still passed out from the drinking the night before. She opened the tent to find him stirring. "Hello father, I have a little surprise for you! Look what I have." Princess pulled out the cash she had received from the distant visitors. Her father looked at her with long eyes. "I am happy for what I did father." She reassured her father over and over. "As long as you're happy my daughter." The Chief picked up the money and kissed it with joy. "Maybe we should invite them for a breakfast gathering." "Good thoughts my wise father." Princess immediately exited the tent with excitement. She ran for the water and on the horizon she could see the boat in the distance, about a mile off the shore. Her body language said it all. She returned to the tribe somber knowing she would not have another opportunity to relive the events again. She joined the rest in celebration in a breakfast feast breaking the news to the members their generous guests have departed. Chief Powow Lee turns to his daughter in the middle of the meal and asks, "What does my daughter want to do with her new found wealth?" "Oh father, you know I do not care what comes of that money. It is for the tribe, for you." "Shall we invest in a car for you? For the tribe if you would like?" "Father, I do not care what comes of the money. You decide."

Meanwhile, Bob and Jeff were sailing the waters, more adventure ahead. Though they were thinking about the times to come they were also thinking of the past and what they have left behind. Back in Consecon Bob's wife is in deep conversation with Sargent Dan Morrison which was leading the case involving her husband Bob and his brother Jeff. They have seen each other many times in relation to the case however it was turning into more of a relaxed relationship; they seemed to take a shining to each other. As they sat at the kitchen table over a cup of tea Katie asked Sargent Dan Morrison for advice to what she should do about the life insurance policy she has on her husband. "You can't legally cash out on the life policy because Bob Thorton is not legally dead at this time. You will have to wait a minimum of 3 years without contact for him to be declared dead." "Well, I have a little bit of money in the bank so I should be able to make it. Perhaps I should sell the farm. I should be able to get a pretty penny out of this place. If I sell it in the spring then I should be able to live for a couple years with no worries. Bob's mother has also offered to help me with a little money if I need." As they walked around the property they talked like friends, perhaps not just friends. They became to know each other a little more after each visit. Sargent Dan Morrison's advances became more known Katie. "Would you like to join me for dinner in town some time?" "I would like that" Katie glanced at him out of the corner of her eye with a smile spread across her face. "What about now?" "Tonight?" "Why not? I don't have any plans. Do you?" "No." "Well then? What do you say?" "Yes!" Katie said with no hesitation. Katie made her way back to the house to freshen up. She offered the Sargent a beer while he waited for her to get ready. The Sargent politely sat at the kitchen table, where most of Katie and Bob's fights originated, ironic don't you think? Katie appeared in the door way with a flowing white dress which stopped right above her knee, showing just enough to draw the attention of Dan. The Sargent stood at attention when Katie made her appearance, simply overwhelmed by her beauty. Her skin was like porcelain and her makeup accented just the right spots on her face, not to mention her eyes. Dan extended his hand to Katie as any gentleman would. Katie was not used to this behavior extended toward her however she loved every moment of it. Her checks blushed with red as she took his hand and followed him out of the house. Bob was no longer a thought. As Katie entered the car she was comfortable, they drove to town with no silence, there was no grasping for words. Katie rested her hand on the middle console and Dan took the opportunity to express his intentions toward her by resting his hand upon hers, causing her heart to begin to race. All Katie could think about at that moment was, is there going to be a kiss at the end of the night? Is he going to want to stay the night? What am I going to do if this is going to turn into something? What will people think? Katie exiled all these thoughts immediately and embraced the handsome, charming man sitting beside her. They arrived at Jim's, one of the nicest, busiest restaurants in Trenton. Dan helped Katie out of the car and held her close all the way to the entrance. She felt important, wanted, a feeling she was unfamiliar with. As they approached the hostess stand Katie heard, "Sargent? You don't have a reservation tonight do you?" "No, I am afraid not, however I was wondering if there is any room for myself and this beautiful young lady?" "Of course, anything for one of the towns finest." They were immediately escorted into the restaurant to a small table with privacy, practically hidden from the other patrons. They sat during dinner, enjoying the conversation as well as the food. As the dinner came to an end they gathered their items and made their way out the door. When Dan dropped off Katie he asked her to stay in the car. Dan made his way over to the passenger side and opened the door for Katie, took her hand and helped her out of the car. Katie was visibly nervous. He eased her worries by taking her arm and walking her to the door. Katie leaned towards him while standing in front of the door, pressing her lips to his. Dan pulled away from her soft lips and asked her to go out again. He left with the promise of calling her soon.

Meanwhile, Jeff and Bob were sailing toward Kenora, on the edge of Manitoba and Ontario. The land of a thousand lakes. As they arrive in Kenora they were looking for a populated dock to pull into, the worst thing is to look obvious at this point. As they tied the boat up, Jeff walked to the Dock Manager and asked as politely as possible if they were able to park there for a little while. Jeff explained they were on a trip to the West coast and they would no longer require the services of this boat. "Do you know any dealerships or anyone looking to purchase a fine boat? We would greatly give you a very handsome commission." "Actually I know a gentleman which would love to look at the boat. Give me a minute lassie and I will make a call." The manager walked into his office, closed the door and picked up the phone. As he strolled out of his office the manager looked at Jeff and said, "How much are you looking to sell that beauty for?" "Between $3000-4000." "And my commission will be 20%?" "I think we will be able to work something out." "Then you must be looking for a car? How about I trade you straight up for my car, a Pontiac Lemanz 1950." The manager dangles the keys in front of Jeff with a big smile. "Give me a minute." Jeff turned on his heals to approach Bob. Bob was still struggling to tie up the boat. "Bob! This guy wants us to trade him straight up for his car, a Pontiac Lemanz 1950. What do you say?" "Well, we can go check out the car and go from there. Fuck your fast! I have not even finished tying up the boat and you have sold it for a new car." The boys walked up to the gentleman propositioning them to trade the boat for the car. "Show us your car mister and we will see if we have a deal." The man pointed to the Dark Blue mint condition Pontiac Lemanz 1950 and said, "Have a look at it!" They walked over to the car, checked out all around it to ensure there was no body damage which could potentially get them pulled over by the cops on the road. They opened up the doors and sat in starting the engine to hear a purr. Bob abruptly said, "Let's close this fucking deal and get the fuck on our way to Winnipeg little brother!" They exited the car with confidence and strutted towards the dock master. "You have a deal sir! All I ask is for the ownership to be signed over to John and Grant Smith. Here are the keys to the boat. Happy sailing!" The boat master expressed he wished them to discard the licence plates as soon as they get into another province. Bob and Jeff agreed to the conditions and the pen hit the car registration. Bob and Jeff turned on their toes and climbed into the car bringing with them their duffle bag and all belongings they would use on the road. As they began to pull away with the windows open and the freedom in their hair the dock master yelled to them, "Where you boys headed anyways?" "The open road sir! The open road." With a polite wave the boys were headed out of town.

A couple miles down the road Jeff and Bob come to the Manitoba boarder. Once they approached the boarder they saw a line of traffic stopped, being checked. They began to sweat, worry about the next few minutes and if this was the end of the trip. Suddenly they noticed to the right all cars were going straight through. On the left all the trucks had to stop and be checked before they left the province. A sigh of relief escaped them both as they realized they were in the clear this time. But, how long were they going to be this lucky? When would they be stopped by the authorities? It was inevitable wasn't it? Jeff looked at Bob with a grin on his face "Boy we sure are lucky aren't we brother?" Bob smiled in response.

Their luck didn't run well for long as 3 miles past the border Jeff and Bob seen cherry red and blue sirens up ahead. "Jeff! What are we going to do? These cops are stopping every car that's passing by." "We just have to keep our cool Bob; I don't think they're looking for us anymore, there was probably an accident up ahead. Don't worry just stay calm." As Jeff and Bob pulled up to the officer waiving them down, they noticed both their hands were extremely sweaty. "What happened over here officer?" asked Jeff, "Listen boys, the weather up ahead is one of the biggest storm we've seen in a long time. There is no need to drive up any further. You won't be able to see a thing. There is a motel called "Borderline" just half a mile west, we are advising everyone to get off the road immediately and head there for a safe night. We don't need any unneeded accidents right guys?" Said the officer, he didn't look like he was in any mood to be joked around with. "We will advise the motel tomorrow when it will be clear enough for everyone to continue on their way." "We could use a good night's rest and a hot meal, thanks for the heads up officer. We will head straight there." Said a nervous Jeff, "You have yourselves a good night guys!" "You as well sir!" Bob and Jeff drove off not believing their luck today. They were hoping this luck stays with them.

When Jeff and Bob pull up to the motel, they notice it's actually quite a nice motel, they wouldn't be surprised if it was filled with tons of hot women wanting to stay clear of the storm. A smiled appeared of both their faces as they secretly read each other's mind.

As the guys walk into the motel, they look all around them in surprise. The walls were white as snow, the place was clean they must have regular maintenance on site. Not like most motels in the area. They noticed a beautiful brunette smiling at them from the receptionist counter. "Hello! Welcome to the Borderline gentleman, how may I help you this evening?" She had the most beautiful eyes with Bridget Bardo kind of lips. "We were advised by an officer a couple miles east from here. Apparently there is a huge storm coming and we would like a safe place for the night." Jeff said with a wink. "I can surely help you, would you like a double bed or single?" She said puzzled. "Definitely one room each ma'am and maybe a nice discount for us since we did have to drive all this way up here." Said Bob pushing Jeff out of the way. "I'll see what I can do" she said while winking back at Bob. "That will be room 107 and 108, there is a small coffee shop down the hall to the right where you can get a fresh hot meal, as well as a couple of drinks if you are looking for a good time." "Perfect! Maybe we will get to bump into you later on, why don't you come join us for a drink?" Said Bob hoping to close the deal. "My break is in an hour, maybe I'll catch you guys there." "What is your name?" Said Bob before walking away, "The name's Candy." "I guess they knew you would turn out to be sweet" Said Bob as Jeff was yanking him away already bored and annoyed that he lost this one. Hopefully this motel was filled with other hot women.

After a nice hot fresh shower, the guys decide to get dressed and go for a hot meal. They had to make sure they looked clean and smelled good if they wanted to get lucky tonight.

On their way to the coffee shop Bob starts going through everything in his head. There is always time for fun but you have to make sure all your points are covered for sure if you want to succeed. "Should we leave the money in the car? Or should we hide it in the bedroom?" Asked Bob. "I don't think it's a good idea to be moving all that money into the room. I didn't see many places we could hide all that cash besides if I can get lucky tonight I'm bringing back a woman and you know how much I trust a woman around my money. Definitely don't want them near each other." "Good thinking Jeff, okay let's forget our troubles for the night and go enjoy ourselves." Bob patted Jeff on the back as they silently agreed to not mention it again for the night.

They get to the coffee shop and each order a medium-rare steak with baked potatoes, lots of sour cream on the side of course and row of 7 shots of Zambooka. They were ready to forget their troubles tonight. As they are finishing their dinner they notice Candy walking into the coffee shop. God she was beautiful. Very curvaceous in all the right spots. She noticed the guys right away, but walked to the bar instead. "Playing hard to get I see" Said Bob even more turned on. She waived the bartender over and whispered something in her ear. The bartender smiled over at the guys and said something back to her with a wink. Candy made her way over to the guys "How you boys liking the motel?" "The cook can definitely serve a great meal!" said Bob shooting back a shot. The bartender walked over with a tray of tequila shots "This one's on the house guys" "Guys meet my friend Tammy. We have worked together for about 6 years now." Jeff automatically reached out for her hand "You are a beauty, please tell me you are going to tell those lame guys in the back to take over and come join us." Without another word Tammy pulled herself up a seat next to Jeff "My shift is basically done I'm sure those guys can handle it from here." As the night went on, and shots got re-ordered over and over both couples were starting to become a little tipsy and interested in each other. It's almost about midnight now and Candy realizes she needs to close up the front. "I need to lock all the doors, and make sure everything is secure, but I'm so drunk I probably can't even stick the key into the key whole at this point." She looked at Bob with a pout. "I can definitely help you out with that, don't you worry. Guys we will see you tomorrow, we are going to close up the front."Said Bob while shooting back another shot. "See you tomorrow Bob,you two have fun." Tammy said "hold on you guys" she walks over to the bar and comes back pulling out a two bottles of Bailey's from underneath her shirt. "This is to make sure you guys keep warm tonight" she said with a grin. "We will make sure we put this to good use, here's some money for all the great hospitality tonight." Bob said handing Tammy over a couple of fifty dollar bills. Tammy's eyes opened up and she said thank you. This must have been the best tip she's received in all the 6 years she's been working at the Borderline.

By the time Candy and Bob got to the reception, they couldn't keep their hands off each other. They got to the desk and Bob picked Candy up and sat her on the desk as he kissed every inch of her neck. Candy immediately took off his shirt by ripping the buttons apart. They wanted each other so bad, adrenaline and heat pumping through their veins. "You are so beautiful Candy, your body is amazing." Said Bob as he caressed every beautiful curve she had. "Take me Bob, show me just how beautiful I really am" and with that, Bob thrust himself into her, over and over. Each push deeper and harder as Candy moaned his name louder and louder. Candy made Bob feel like a king. She had this mystery about herself but made sure Bob knew exactly what wanted all at the same time. Her breast were massive, double D's, they could hardly fit in Bob's hands. This made Bob get even hungrier for her. He began caressing her breasts as he thrust into her with so much force the table began to move. Candy couldn't take it anymore. She dug her nails in his back pulling him closer and closer as she began moaning Bob's name in his ear. Bob grunted in the moment of ecstasy sealing the deal with one last thrust. Candy pulled him towards her "that was amazing. You knew exactly how to make me nuts for you." "You make me nuts with your sexiness. What do you say we lock this place up and go to my room. You sure know how to tire a guy out" said Bob with a wink. Candy giggled and pulled herself off the desk. They made sure to put the table back, close all the doors, and headed back to the room, drunk, tired and happy.

Jeff and Bob met in the lobby the next morning. The guys had a serious hangover but after a nice shower they felt refreshed and ready to hit the road again. Jeff seemed really eager to leave but Bob made sure to be a gentleman and say goodbye to Candy as they were checking out. "So if you guys are ever in the area again, you know where to find me" said Candy looking only at Bob. "Believe me, this will be the first place I come to" "Yeah, yeah it was nice meeting you Candy!" interrupted Jeff while yanking Bob's arm. On their way out, Bob got angry and said "what the fuck is the matter with you? I wasn't done talking to her!" "This place is a dump. You had your fun cowboy let's hit the road" said Jeff before slamming the car doors. Bad night? Looks like Mr. Ladies Man didn't have such a great time last night. Bob got into the car, started the engine and began chuckling "let me guess...that time of the month?" "No! She was just lazy and lame. Lay there like a sack of potatoes. She wouldn't even give a blowjob. So I busted a nut and went straight to bed. Should've gone for that girl sitting at the table across from us. She winked at me at one point when Tammy went to the washroom

, you know." Said Jeff trying to cheer himself up "I don't want to make you jealous so I won't give you the details of my night because I had one hell of a night. You should see my back!" said Bob lighting up a cigarette still chuckling. "Screw you. When we get to Winnipeg I'll show you." Bob just kept chuckling. "My night was fuzzy though. Bob how much did you tip Tammy last night? I don't even know how much dinner was. We should do a count of the money, if we're going to blow this money we got to be smart from the beginning." Jeff got the bag of cash from the backseat and began counting. Bob took another drag of his cigarette and said "I gave her $150 bucks. The dinner was only $60. I knew I screwed up as soon as I saw how much I handed to her. I took one too many 50's and because the bills are so crisp they got stuck. I didn't want to take the 50's back and look like a jerk so I just said what the hell." "Shit, I should be one of your dates, see how well you spoil me!" Said Jeff and he himself lit up a cigarette too. He didn't stress too much over it, I mean after all the guys had all this money they can do whatever they want with it. What's a $150.00 to them now? "Do you think a tip like that would make them question us thought Bob? Should we have used fakes names? I mean it's not every day that two good looking guys like us walk into a motel and tip a waitress $150.00. What if they suspect us and call the cops?" "Whoa take it easy Jeff. First off, the girls wanted sex. We wanted sex. We gave them what they wanted and they're happy. Second, it's been quite some time now and the cop didn't even seem to suspect us at all...why would they even bother suspecting us. And third, no waitress is going to get mad for getting an amazing tip, calling the cops and reporting that she had sex with a man she met at work." Said Bob with a big laugh this time, Jeff seemed to think about these points and realized Bob was right. They were going to be okay. The cop hadn't suspected them at all and as long as they remain smart they will get away with this.

They were now only an hour and a half away from Winnipeg. "When I was in jail, my cellmate told me that when he gets out of jail he's going to go to Winnipeg to change his identity. He ratted on a big time drug dealer and he said there was a ton of guys waiting for him to come out so they can kill him. He said in Winnipeg, they have an underworld where they can change identities." Said Jeff checking out the map. "That's a great idea. But, how would we find these 'underworld guys' and can we trust them?" Jeff answered with "We sure as hell can't trust them. But, my cellmate told me these type of guys hang out in dungy bars on the north end of Winnipeg. On Main Street." "Then I guess that's our next stop. I could use a beer!" said Bob as he began to step on the peddle after turning up the radio.

When they arrive in Winnipeg, they find a bar called "aokley" the men are starved and want a fresh hot meal. The bar was dungy and old. Grease on the walls, and the place smelled of alcohol and cigarettes. "Just try to keep a low profile, if anybody asks us where we're from, just say we are making a pit stop on our vacation." Said Bob. Jeff nodded in agreement. They found a table in the far right corner of the room. It was perfect because it allowed us to stay clear from everyone but they were able to see everyone in the bar at the same time. Jeff decided to order some drinks and get a menu, he walked up to the bar and called the bartender over. "Two shots of whiskey, and do you have a menu?" "we only service chicken fingers and fries." The man looked so dirty, his apron was filled with grease. "Uh sure, that will work,i'll have an order of two please." Said Jeff. "I haven't seen you two around here before, i know everybody in this town." Said the bartender. "Uh yeah, we are just passing by, we needed a place to eat, we are on vacation." "Hmm, i don't think you are,i mean two fellas on vacation such as yourselves would probably want to find a much upscale place to eat." The bartender said with a very sly smile, his teeth were as yellow as the walls of the bar. He placed the two shots of wiskey on the counter and slided them towards Jeff. "Thanks boss, i'll let you know if we need anything else." Said Jeff picking up the glasses, he noticed he was starting to get nervous. The whole vacation idea was obviously not the best to use. "My name is Joe. If you two fellas need anything, don't hesitate to let me know. I know everybody in this town. And i can also always smell wa lie when i see one." He said extending out his hand for a shake. Nervous Jeff shook his hand with Joe, "what makes you think I,m lying to you?" "Come on fella, look around you. You are in a pretty bad place here, why would you choose this place instead off everywhere else." "Well to be honest, maybe you can help us out. You see, we're from Kansas and we're trying to get a Canadian passport so we could work here." "Ahh! Now i finally get some honesty. Well i could help you out you know. But everything comes at a good price." Said Joe with a wink. Jeff wasn't sure why, but for the first time in a long time he felt a little safe. Maybe its because it was the first time he had told a little truth to someone other then Bob. "What would be your price?" asked jeffgetting comfortable. "$300 cash."Said Joe without any reaction in his face. "You're a serious business man, but alright, if what you are saying is true. $300 sounds alright." "Well there is a place around here, on 369 Main Street. About a block south from here, there is a gentleman that could help you out with your problem. He is a Chinese man that goes by 'sir.' Don't try to call him anything else. He is very high maintenance and will not do business with you if you don't show him the respect he wants. When you go to his door, tell him Monty sent you. It will keep him from slamming the door in your face. He doesn't really like people." "Well I appreciate all the information Joe, give me a moment while I talk this over with my brother." "Not so quick, I gave you the information, now pay up. $300 was the deal I believe." Jeff reached into his pocket and pulled out the money. He felt good about this, but he was hoping Monty was telling the truth otherwise Bob was going to be one angry man. He walked back to Bob and explained to him what just happened. "Well, that's definitely quick progress brother, you were supposed to just grab a drink but I'm happy." Said Bob shooting back a shot of whiskey. The gentleman decided to finish up their meal, and head over to see "sir."

A block south of the bar, they found a door with small "369" in gold little numbers. Jeff knocked on the door but both brothers heard nothing. "Bet you the scum bag lied. There doesn't seem to be anyone here. What if an old lady ends up walking out?" Said Bob. "Relax, let me try one more time." Jeff knocked on the door a second time and to his surprise the door swung open and they saw a

Near Perfect Getaway

middle aged Chinese man filled with tattoos from head to toe. "What do you want?!" he said while taking a drag off a cigarette. "Umm, my name is Jeff and this is Bob. We're sorry to bother you "sir" but Monty from "Oakley" bar up the street sent us here. He told us you could help us change our identity." Bob shot Jeff a look that screamed "You idiot!!!" Sir just stood there, and eyed them from head to toe. "Are you cops?" "Oh no, far from it "sir," we are from Kansas city and we just want to work in Canada legally. Kansas is not very good in the job market at this time." Said Bob trying to smooth things out, "we are willing to pay for this of course. Name your price." His eyes brightened up. "I can help you out, but the price is steep." He took another drag of his cigarette. "Trust me, this means a lot to us. Name your price" said Bob with a stern look in his eye. "Come inside" he swung his door opened to reveal and cigarette smoke filled room with a couch and tv. He closed the door but not before making sure there was nobody watching. "Well, you don't look like cops. And if you end up to be, you'll be dead in about 24 hours, so I guess I can trust you." He took another puff of his cigarette, "what type of ID's are you looking to get?" "Well we want a full identity change. We will need a Canadian Passport, Driver's Licence and Birth Certificates." Jeff was taking over at this point. He knew they were in a good place now, they weren't planning on ripping him off so they should remain alive. "1000" he took another drag while folding his arms, "how long will it take to be done?" asked Bob, "2 days. You pick it up here. But if I see anything I don't like, or you make me think I can't trust you, I destroy them" "okay" said Jeff and with that, reached into his pocket and held out $500 dollars. "500 now, and 500 when we pick it up." "Sir" snatched the money "follow me" he led them downstairs to a basement. Inside the was a camera set up to face a white canvas. "Alright, have you thought of what names you want?" "Yes Bob is going to be 'Grant Bigby' and I will be 'John Bigby.'"

Sir took their pictures and took down their information. The gentleman finished up and agreed to meet him again in exactly two days.

They rented a motel both nights but were already looking for an apartment to get once their identities have been changed. They had found one they liked, a little two bedroom on the east side of town, very quiet, they agreed to go see it after they picked up their new identities. Two days later the brothers returned to see Sir and were very relieved to see that their new identities were finished and looked very real. Sir seemed happy to see that he could trust them. He even offered for them to come over some time for shots of whiskey. With this type of weapon in their hands they are able to get an apartment and look for a job and make this all finally work out.

"Let's get it John!" said Bob looking around their two bedroom apartment. It was clean, and had just been refurbished. Not the best job, but definitely better than the other ads they had seen in the local newspapers the last two days. They each had their own bedroom with their own washroom. The kitchen had all new appliances, a brand new fridge and stove. (Not like the guys would use the stove though. They preferred to use the microwave for most of their meals.) The walls were pearl white and all the furniture was covered in a light-mint. A bit girly, but definitely better than any other apartment they had seen. But it didn't come cheap. In fact it cost the guys $100 a month rent. They knew they had to find a job. And fast.

A couple of weeks had passed but the guys had no luck finding any job. Until one morning, on their regular job hunting hour which was always done during breakfast, John stumbled across an ad in the newspaper for snow plowing. This is Winnipeg, there is always snow here, finding a job in this field definitely had its benefits. "Lion's snow Removal – hiring machine operators, season begins December 1st." "That's in two weeks!" "Well let's give them a call and see if the job is still available" said john while picking up the phone and dialing the digits.

"Make sure you don't screw this up now! Your name is John and I'm Grant." After a moment John got off the phone with a huge grin on his face. "We have an interview at 4 o'clock today! At 764 Harver Street." "Okay, from now on, whenever we speak to each other we need to say your fake names first. Until we get into the habit of responding to them and saying them." Said Grant pacing around the room half filled with excitement and half filled with worry. They were doing great, after all nobody has asked any questions and nobody has any suspicions but Grant wonders if the lack of people in their circle has been the leading cause of why they have been able to get away with everything. The moment you add people to a problem, the same moment you must add all the questions they will probably ask. Where are they from? How old are they? Why aren't they married? With time every question will arise. And the only way they can make sure their safety is by being prepared for each question they will face.

The guys earned themselves a job in Lion's snow Removal. It didn't take much. Their job interview consisted of a simple questionnaire and pamphlet with complete instructions of how to operate a bob cat. The guys had driven bob cats plenty of times throughout their lives and once they mentioned it, it was the icing on top of the cake. They worked 40 hour weeks for $1.00 an hour. The guys went home every night and began thinking of new ideas to make their past lives seem more believable. John was a playboy in his younger years, fathered a daughter back home to a woman named Casey who was a n one night stand gone wrong. Now he's trying to save up enough to send some money for his daughter. Grant was a mechanic back home. He's always been too focused on school to pay attention to women. He played a more shier type. He let Grant do most of the talking, and tried to avoid anyone that crossed his path the first chance he got. This was mostly because John had a tendency to be the more outgoing of the two brothers. The problem with that was, once John gets talking, he starts to talk too much. Especially when there is liquor involved. Grant on the other hand, was sharp. Grant was always on the ball. He could come up with a lie on the spot, and every sentence he ever spoke around their so called "co-workers" was thought-out in his head at least 10 times before it escaped his mouth.

It was a cold night in December. They were working a night shift. It was -35 degrees below 0. The city seemed empty at this time of night. Everyone was home bundled up, either drinking coffee or drinking something bitter to warm themselves up. The winter was here and that meant many snow storms. The type that drop 10 degrees within a span of 5 hours. This was one of those nights. The men were shivering. Grant's bob cat had broken down twice that night and he was beginning to get anxious. He hadn't worked so hard to get away with this plan to stay living in a small city filled with knuckleheads who wanted to lie and cheat their way through everything. Grant didn't like Winnipeg. He wanted to be somewhere hot. Somewhere you can wake up in the morning and think you are blessed to be able to see such a beautiful sight. A place where the weather didn't freeze you to the bone, and a place that had some hot woman! The woman in this town resembled Sasquatch more than an Audrey Hepburn. No Winnipeg wasn't cutting it." "John are you there?" radio'd Grant. "Yeap! Man don't tell me your machine broke down again! I am not leaving this machine for another minute tonight!" "No, I got a better idea. What do you say we call it quits? You know, go for another road trip. I mean, we do have a ton of cash, it's been months since anyone has heard anything about the case, and besides we've been here long enough, we should start to make a move now to the west."

It was Saturday morning, the guys made sure to get their paycheques on Friday because they weren't about to work for free, didn't matter how much money they had. The world was a cruel place and they had to be just as

Near Perfect Getaway

cruel to survive. The weather was bitter cold. "Man I can't wait to get out of here. My fingers feel like icicles." Said Grant packing the last pieces of clothing into his suitcase. "Let's hit the road and get on out of here" said John. The guys hopped into their car, and hit the road. The drive up to Regina was going to take about a day. "Slow down John, there is a cop behind you." Said Grant while checking his passanger mirror. "Oh Shit, I'm going 20 km over. I'm trying to slow down without making it obvious." Said John while staring into his rear view mirror and noticing that the cop is looking right at them. It was too late. The cop put his sirens on and the guys knew they were in trouble. They pulled over immediately "Now keep your cool, and make sure you don't mess up with your identity." Said Grant looking very nervous. The cop got out of the car. He was a bald headed man with a huge gut. Clearly he was the type who ate donughts every day. He walked over slowly and when he approached the car he bent over so that he was eye to eye with John. "You off in a hurry there?" He said with a toothpick on the side of his mouth. "Sorry sir, we're not in a rush at all. My feet are so cold I guess I lost feeling of how hard I was pushing the pedal. I will make sure this doesn't happen again." "Licence and registration please." This cop was not in a good mood. Grant knew one wrong word and he would question everything about them. John took the licence out of his glove box and handed it over to the cop. "Where are you guys headed?" Said the cop while looking at his driver's licence. "We are on our way to Regina sir, do you happen to know any spot there where I could bring this car to get it looked at. The snow's been messing with my wheels." Said John quickly trying to change the subject. "There's a spot called "Larry's Auto shop" it's located at the first set of lights as soon as you hit Regina. But I can't help you out today. You were 20km over and I have to write you out a ticket. It's going to be $40.00. You can pay it once you get to Regina." Said the cop hanging them the ticket. "Thank you officer, we will make sure we get this paid as soon as we reach our destination." Said Grant trying to take control of the conversation. "You guys have a safe trip and make sure you slow down!" The cop yelled this out as he was walking away. "Geez, that was close. What a prick! I mean we have a new licence now and a ton of cash but a $40.00 ticket for 20km over you know that guy hates his job." Said John as he was pulling away. "John we are convicts on the run. A $40.00 ticket I can take any day over getting caught and going to jail." Said Grant as he was sparking up a cigarette. His nerves were making his blood boil, and John was beginning to annoy him with his complains. He still had another 3 hours to listen to him so he decided he was going to nap half the way there and then they could switch.

"John wake up! We're here and I'm starving. Let's find a little restaurant and get ourselves a hot meal. My toes are frozen." John woke up and opened his eyes "Man, I had a good dream. A hot blonde and a nice hot beach. Waking up is like a nightmare. Look at these windows. They're basically frozen." Said John as he began rolling down the window and realized it took a couple of pulls of the lever before the ice around the window broke off. "The heater isn't working either John, we have to pay that stupid ticket and get this car fixed. The weather isn't going to be getting any better and I don't feel like freezing my ass off every time we decide to further our adventure." Said Grant, still irritated because he has been driving for over 6 hours and is frozen to the bone. He couldn't wait until everything came together for them. No more being paranoid about getting caught and being able to wake up with a relief instead of that nasty feeling in his stomach that never seemed to leave. "There's the garage the cop was talking about" said John pointing to a really old yellow sign with big blue letters that said "Larry's Auto Shop." This seemed to cheer Grant up a little bit. Finally one thing they can cross off their list. The guys dropped of the car at Larry's and after a close examination from Larry they learned the thermostat in the car was broken. Larry told them the car would be ready first thing tomorrow morning which meant they had to spend another night in a hotel before they could head on down to Calgary. "Do you boys have a place to stay for the night or are you just in town visiting?" said Larry wiping his greasy fingers on his dark blue coveralls and taking a bite out of a tuna fish sandwich. "No, we were actually heading to Calgary but we got a ticket on the way and realized our car wasn't working properly. The cop told us about your shop and told us we could also pay our ticket here. "Oh, must have been Kevin! He's always sending people down to our shop down here. He's been my best friend since high school. He's a good fella." "yes he was very helpful, minus the ticket we got but I guess we can't blame him for that one." Said John after Grant gave him an evil stare which mean shut your mouth. "Well there's a motel a couple of blocks down from here I can give you guys a lift. It's -40 out right now and a walk in this weather is not such a good idea. Especially since you won't pay me for my work until tomorrow morning so I have to make sure you survive the night." Said Larry which a chuckle. His breath smelled like tuna at this point which grossed the guys out and made them hungry at the same time. "Well, don't you worry about your pay, thank you for the ride offer we will definitely take you up on that." Said Grant following Larry to his pick up truck.

Larry dropped the guys off at the "Victoria Inn" and wished them a safe night. The motel was more fancier then the guys expected. It had cream stone walls and lots of chandeliers. The maid walked by, a gorgeous redhead with bright red lips to match her hair. The guys definitely liked what they saw of this place. They checked in and headed straight to the restaurant. Grant ordered a medium rare steak with a glass of red wine. He wanted to match the atmosphere and decided not to drink like a shmuck for the night. John himself also felt in the mood to be classy and joined Grant on the wine decision with a nice medium-rare roast beef. The food smelled delicious and so did the waitress. The guys haven't ate food this good since they left home. It made them feel good. After dinner, they ordered another couple of glasses of wine and decided to head back to their room. John was tired and fell asleep quickly but Grant being on the ball like he always was decided to go through some of the newspapers that were in the lobby of Victoria Inn. He came back to the room, sat on his bed and began reading. The first 3 newspapers had nothing too interesting for Grant. One man shot, a woman missing and a rapist on the run a few miles down the road. But as he kept flipping through the magazines he saw one that caught his eye. It read "Northern News" which covered British Columbia, Alberta and Saskatchewan. As he began flipping through the pages he came across real estate ads and one in particular caught his eye. The ad read "American Millionaire buys abandoned resort in northern B.C. for $8,000,000" as Grant kept reading the ad he saw that the millionaire is looking for investors for the property. It was a ski resort, 300 acres with a lake, mountain ski hills, golf course, hotel, has a 20 bed hospital log and over a dozen cabins with a restaurant and ski shops. He is looking to extend the resort with more accommodations. Grant's eyes lit up as he finished reading the ad. This was music to his ears. He couldn't wait to wake up John and tell him all about it. This was music to his ears and he knew John was going to be ecstatic. Grant was going to wait a couple more hours before waking up John as he knew how grumpy John was when woken up. In the meantime he decided to walk over to their mini fridge and drink a couple of whiskey shots while composing a master plan for their lifetime dream resort.

When John woke up the next morning Grant was waiting by the bed with two fresh hot coffees' and a huge smile across his face. "What are you so happy about? Did you get laid when I fell asleep or something?" Said

John taking the coffee from Grant. "You won't believe what I read last night! We have found the answers to our prayers!" Said Grant as he lifted up a newspaper in his hands. John was confused. He wasn't sure what Grant was talking about until he began reading the ad. "John, this place could make us a fortune as well as it has all the things we've been looking for! He wants investors! That's what we will be!" "What makes you think he's going to settle for just two investors. Once you start adding people into the equation you won't be looking at much more profit." Said John skeptical but with a relief deep down at the same time. "We're rich too! If we put a high enough offer for him he won't want anyone else. You see, I've spent all night thinking about this. All we need to buy out is the ski shop and restaurant. We can remodel it all because we can afford it and that alone will bring us revenue for the rest of our lives! Besides do you think a millionaire wants to share too? Why do you think he's a millionaire. John this is the best opportunity we're ever going to find! Look at all the accommodations it has! And it's beautiful over there, there's a lake also and we can make the place so good that all the hot chicks will want to come and vacation with us!" Said Grant dancing around the room like he was a four year old child seeing all the Christmas presents under the Christmas tree first thing in the morning. "Alright! You crazy bastard! I have to admit this is the best idea you've had yet!" said John as he decided to join in Grant's child behaviour and began jumping on the bed. "Let's take off right now! Let's hit the road! Let's start off our lives!" Said John in crazy voice, he was really beginning to picture all of this coming together! "Now hold it there brother. We haven't even ate breakfast yet or picked up our car as a matter of fact. Also, we still need to pay our ticket! And, I think we will seem a lot more professional and cut out chances of competition if we phone him before we head up there to have a professional business meeting." Said Grant while picking up a sweater off the chair and putting it on. "Also, we should come up with a plan and strategy of why we will be an asset to show him that we are serious about this."

The guys headed down to the restaurant, they both ordered eggs and bacon with some orange juice and asked the waitress for some paper and pen. "Alright, we need to make a plan so we know what to say to him." Said Grant as he began to write out "List" on the piece of paper. "Well renovations is a must." Said John with a mouth full of eggs. "Well we have to see the place first to decide what type of renovations they will need but I agree renovations will definitely be a priority. We should also mention that we want to purchase out the restaurant and ski hill. We can upgrade all the ski slopes by doing all the maintenance for the sky buggies, making sure the wires are all secure and intact, we can light up all the buggies and lines so that when people are going up the hill in the buggy they have a nice view as the night draws closer, we will need to build a little shack in which people can buy their tickets at, we will probably need to purchase at least 200 hundred ski boards and ski's, if the business blooms we can always purchase more but it's better to have enough so that we don't run out and cause line ups and irritate people by waiting in line. That will kill the business pretty quickly." Said Grant as his hands were writing all these ideas on the paper faster than rain can come down. "Geez, Grant if I knew you were so good at this business planning I might have just opened up a business with you way back in our early years." Said John while finishing off his orange juice. "And as far as the restaurant, we will need to see the size of it and condition first but I want a restaurant so big that it can easily sit over 200 people. We will hire the best cooks in B.C. and serve top notch food. After all, the food is what keeps people happy after spending the day outside especially on the cold days." "Yeah! We can serve the finest steaks, and the beef that's so juicy it melts on your tongue! And chicken soups so good that you think your grandmother made it for you while you had the stomach flu." Said John with his eyes wide like an owl. "Oh don't you worry brother we will serve the best of the best. Food of all varieties and freshness. These people will love our place so much their kids won't want to leave!." Said Grant "lets order ourselves a shot and celebrate our plans how does that sound John" "excuse me miss, 2 shots of whiskey please" said john to the pretty blonde haired waitress. She returned quickly with two shots waiting for them. "Here's to a bright future!" Said Grant raising his glass "And shit ton of money" finished off John as he clinked Grant's shot. The guys were happy. Finally really happy. For the first time in a long time Grant didn't have that upsetting feeling in his stomach. Like this could all be over in a minute. "Ahhh that was good! Alright, now our next step is to call up this millionaire and convince him that we are right investors!" Said grant while leaving money for their bill as well as a $15.00 tip for the pretty blonde haired waitress.

"Okay, now I'm guessing you're going to do all the talking" Said John as he plopped on the bed. "Yeah, no offence John but I think I can be a bit more persuasive then you" "Fine by me! I like to do as little work as possible, you know this" Said John with a laugh.

Grant began dialing the number "here goes everything" after 3 rings a gentleman picked up the phone

"Hello, Christopher speaking" said the kind voice over the phone. "Hello I am calling about your ad in the 'Northern Newspaper' regarding investors for your property." Said Grant with a firm voice that meant he meant business. "Ah yes, how would you like to invest Mr… ?" "Call me Grant, well me and my brother were interested in investing in the restaurant and Sport shop " "Well it's nice to meet you Grant, I can assure you you won't be sorry. I won't lie, it's going to be pricey, but the land is huge and once I fix everything up there will most definitely be a lot of profit from this resort." "I don't doubt it, from the pictures and information you provided in the ad I have a big vision. I have a bunch of ideas I have gathered together to let you know how we can better your property." "A man who thinks ahead, I like that. Well, I'm in California at the moment I have a bunch of meetings to attend. But I can be available in about 2 weeks to meet you at the resort so that you can check out the property and we can sit down to discuss everything. If you like what you see and you're serious about this investment I will be able to have lawyers down the next day." Said Christopher. "That sounds terrific! I will be there along with my brother John exactly two weeks from today." Said Grant while showing John a thumbs up. "I look forward to meeting you and your brother. You take care" "We look forward to meeting you as well Christopher, you take care now." Said John as he hung up the phone. "We got a meeting with Christopher two weeks from today." Said John as he slapped his knee with his hand in excitement. "No way! He's interested? That's awesome!" "Well, he's looking for investors and by the sounds of it I don't think anyone has put an offer for the restaurant or the sport shop yet because he didn't mention that. He wants to sit down and discuss everything once we meet and see the property." "Yeah that makes sense. No point in a millionaire waisting his time until we see the property and he knows we're serious." Said John as he got up off the bed. "Okay, now we have to check out of this hotel, walk over to Larry's Auto Shop pick up our car and make sure we pay our ticket. Once we settle all of that we can start to head down to Calgary and spend a night there." Said Grant as he began putting away his sweater into his little travel bag. The guys headed downstairs after packing and began walking to Larry's Auto Shop. It was a cold morning, but it wasn't as bad as the last couple of days. The guys felt like weather alone gave them a nice break. After walking in silence for about 10 minutes john began to think to himself of how things were back home. He missed his little sister Julie a whole lot. He didn't mention her but he thought about her every night before he went to bed. He hoped that she was doing okay, and deep down it broke his heart knowing that she thinks they are dead and will never get to see them again. "Grant, do you think there is any way we can let Julie know that we are alive?" Said John with a hoarse voice. "No way, she thinks we are dead. What do you think we can do. Write her a letter with a picture 'Hey here's your dead brothers by the way we're not dead we're criminals on the run. Sorry to have left you grieving and struggling but we're doing fine." Said Grant with sarcasm. "Well, I mean no we don't have to say anything. But maybe there is a way we can at least let her know we are alive. You know how much she looked up to us. You know, give her heart some closure at least." Said John as he began to pick up his pace. He hated when Grant didn't take him seriously. Family at the end of the day was everything to them and after all that they have put them through a little closure wouldn't kill them. "Well how do you propose we pull this idea of yours. I mean how do we let her know we are alive without saying it?" Said Grant, he began to feel bad he could tell this was something John was serious about. And John was usually not the one to be serious. "Well, I have this locket that Sylvia gave to me for my 20th birthday. It opens up with a picture of her and I. I still remember the day she gave it to me. I went home and showed it to Julie and she thought it was the most beautiful gesture.

She really loved that locked. What if I take out the picture of Sylvia and replace the other side with one of yours. Julie will have to know that it was us. Especially since she knows that I was the one who had it. That alone will be enough of a clue to give her closure don't you think?" "Well, that's actually not a bad idea John. But what if she goes to Sylvia and asks her if she sent it to her?" Said Grant, with his mind rolling with all possible outcomes as he always thought of everything before making a decision. "I don't think she will ask Sylvia. Julie is a smart girl. And she always kept our secrets we both know she's not the type to run around town telling everyone. Besides, if we use our real initials in capital letters on the envelope she will put it all together. She was always little a Sherlock Holmes. She can put any puzzle together. " "yeah you're right. I mean worst case scenario, nobody would probably believe her and if she did blab something out to someone, we can send the locket from Calgary while we spend the night there. By the time she gets the locket we will already have left and there will be no way that anyone can trace us back." "This is going to work Grant, I promise you." Said John with a huge smile on his face. "This means a lot to you huh?" "Well yeah, she's our little sister. And I vowed I would always protect her. And since I can't do that right now, knowing I gave her some hope and closure will make me feel a little better. And maybe I will be able to sleep a little better at night." Said John as he began sparking up a cigarette. Grant patted John on the back. "Don't you worry brother. We will make sure we get this done." With that said, about 5 minutes later the guys reached Larry's Auto Shop. Their hands were cold from the frost in the air, they were excited to get their car back. "Hey there fellas! Nice to see you again! Did you walk here form the motel?" "Hey Larry, yeah we walked it didn't take us long. Our legs needed the exercise" Said John with a laugh. "Well, I'm happy to let you know I got the car all fixed up for you guys. I had to replace the thermostat as it was broken and I cleaned out the snow from the tires and breaks. I kept it inside all night and everything that was left behind has melted. She's running like brand new" Said Larry as he handed Grant the keys to the car. "That will be 40 dollars, but probably still a lot less then what you guys spent on the hookers last night." Said Larry with a huge chuckle. The guys began to laugh "Hey, they were worth every penny" Said john going along with the joke. Grant handed Larry $50.00 and said that's for your trouble and the ride you provided us. We really appreciate your help." "Anytime guys, if you're ever back in town make sure you stop to say hello, even if your car isn't having problems." Said Larry with a wink. "Will do! You take care now!"

And with that, the guys jumped into the car, and it started right away. "Feels good to be in a car again. I'm not a big walker" Said John with a laugh. They pulled out of the shop and began heading west towards the post office to pay the ticket. Grant made John go inside and handle the ticket. "Why does it have to be me?" Said John with a grumpy voice. "Well why do I always have to take care of everything? You're the ugly one that's why. Do something!" Said Grant with a laugh. When John returned back to the car he confirmed the ticket was handled with and the guys began their journey down to Calgary.

The drive was about 8 hours but to John it felt like forever. He was happy Grant agreed to send the locket. He just wanted his sister to have some reassurance and he knew once all of it was handled he would feel some relief in his heart himself. Each mile felt like a day to John. But finally, the guys arrived. They stopped at a motel called "Cannille Inn" and checked themselves in. Calgary was a beautiful place. The scenery was gorgeous, filled with hillsides in every direction. Such a peaceful place. The kind you would want to start a family in. And a bonus for the guys, was that there was a ton of beautiful women. Grant already spotted about 5 hot smoking cowgirls within the first 2 miles of reaching Calgary. But they both knew they were here for the night to do the business and then it was off to Vancouver where they really planned to enjoy themselves.

The guys stepped into their motel room, dropped their bags and decided to call room service. "I need a drink!" Said John as he headed towards the bathroom. They didn't feel like going to the restaurant as they didn't want to be seen just in case anything ever got traced back, the less people who seen them the less information the police would have. John decided he wanted a bottle of red wine to ease his mind. Grant made the call and ordered some cheese and crackers along with the wine. Room service was up in their room within 10 minutes and they gave a $5.00 tip which made the man extremely happy. "If you need anything else, please don't hesitate to call the front desk" said the room service waiter with a big smile on his face. "Thank you, now that you mention it do you think you could get us a little box? We have some things we have bought for our families and we would like to store them in something other then a bag. As you can see, we only have our luggage with us." Said Grant, quick to think of a lie on the spot. "That will be no problem at all sir. I have a small wooden box at the front desk that's been empty, I've been using it for paper clips but I can always store them somewhere else." "That is very kind of you sir, here's something extra for your trouble." Said Grant as he slipped him another $2.00. Within 5 minutes the room service attendant was at their door with a wooden box. He thanked the gentleman for their kind tip and headed back downstairs.

John took the locket out of his wallet where he stored it in the pocket meant for change. He took an old picture out of Grant's wallet that he always carried with him. It was picture from their early teens that their father took of them when they were 18. The men stood by their front door; the picture was taken on the night of their prom. John took a pair of scissors and cut out Grant's face. He made sure it was small enough to fit into the locket. It ended up being a perfect fit. "What do you think Grant? At least this is a good picture of you!" "Yeah that picture was taken way before I started getting all my wrinkles. Definitely can't go wrong with that." Said Grant as he put his hands under his chin as to imitate a woman who is confident of her beauty. John let out a chuckle and placed the locket into the box. "We should put a sock into the box to place the locket on. If the mailman gets bored and jiggles the box, it might damage it." Said Grant as he took out a clean pair of socks out of his luggage and placed it under the locket. "That's a good idea Grant." After sealing up the box with some tape, the guys went downstairs, stopped by the little gift shop and luckily were able to find some wrapping paper. They headed back upstairs and wrapped the box so that you could not tell what it was. Once they finished wrapping they began writing their initials on the envelope in capital letters to give Julie a clue. They wrote "Jacob and Bart" and made sure that the J & B were extra big to stand out. Then they went downstairs and asked the room service attendant where the nearest post office was. It was about 3 blocks away and the guys decided to walk it.

Once they got to the post office they asked the post man how much it would cost to send it to Picton, Ontario. "We are going to be mailing this to a box number 389" The post man took the box and began weighing it, "That will be 89 cents." Said the post man as he stamped the package. Grant took a dollar out of his pocket and paid. "Thank you very much sir." As soon as they walked out of the post office John let out a sigh of relief. "Man am I happy we did that! I can literally feel the weight lift off my shoulders. Julie will be shocked and happy!" John was so relieved he even hugged Grant. He was taken aback by this but hugged him back "It's okay brother. We will see her someday. I promise you that. For now God is looking over her and she will get the message we were trying to let her know." John shook his head in agreement and patted his brother back. Then the two walked back to the motel without another word. As if silence in the air did all the emotional talking for them.

That night, John went to bed hoping to have a good night's sleep. Something he hasn't had in about 2 years. He dreamed about Julie. It was almost like a faint memory that he put away in his mind. They were both little, Julie was only 3 and they were playing on their father's tractor. Julie loved climbing up and jumping down into John's hands. "Again, again!" she would yell as she would jump up and down with a smile as big as the sun. John picked her up enough so she could step on the tractor and she would begin to climb up to the hood of the tractor. They did this for hours. John loved seeing her sister smile. But at as she stepped on the step, she went to grab the handle she would use to steady herself but her hand slipped. She fell straight down. John wasn't able to catch her fast enough and she fell with all her weight on her right ankle. Screams filled the sky. It had just happened but her foot was already beginning to swell after a close examination from John. "Shh, I'm going to bring you to mom. Just hang in there Julie. You will be alright. I promise" Said John as he picked his sister up in his arms and began running towards the house. "It hurts! It hurts! Make it go away!" she screamed as she put her head into his chest and soaked it with tears. John came bursting through the side door "Mom! Mom! Julie is hurt! Mom!" His mother appeared from the kitchen with her eyes as big as an owl. "What happened?! Is she okay?" She said running over and grabbing Julie from John and placing her on top of their dinner table. "We were playing on the tractor and she fell. It happened so fast mom I didn't know what to do." Said John as he to began to cry. It hurt him to know that his sister was in pain. He felt responsible and careless. "How many times have I told you not to play on the tractor! Your sister's ankle is sprained. I'm going to grab some ice. You stay with her and calm her down." She walked away towards the kitchen but by her tone and her walk John knew his mother was very angry. She returned with an ice pack and took a face wash towel and wrapped it around Julie's ankle. "You have to be more careful Bob. You're Julie's big brother. She's too young to be able to play the way you do. You need to be more responsible before something worse happens. And if I ever catch the two of you on that tractor again I will spank you both!" She said this with a very stern voice and John and Julie both knew they will never go near that tractor to play again. John stood there and watched the tears streaming down Julie's face. He vowed to himself that for as long as he lives he will protect his sister. He will never let her be hurt ever again. He was going to be there any time she needed him. John suddenly woke up panting. He looked over at the clock next to him and it read 2:30 a.m. He was soaked in sweat. He got these type of dreams often. But they weren't so much dreams as memories. Things he hadn't remembered in a long time seemed to creep up in his dreams. So vivid. Bringing back all the emotions he buried away. He got up to have a glass of water. Grant was snoring away on his bed. He sat on the edge of his bed for some time thinking of his life and his choices before he decided to turn shut off his brain and try to get some sleep. Tomorrow was a new day. A new chance. One day he would be able to turn everything around.

It's now beginning of March of 1953. And things back home in Pickton started to happen. The ice was beginning to melt off everything and winter was coming to an end. One day, while Sylvia was preparing lunch she heard a knock at the door. It was two policeman. "Hello Ma'am." Greeted one of them "I am officer Justin Sparow and this is my partner Jason McCrow. We are dealing with your husband's case and we wanted to come by and tell you in person that with all the sun we're having these days the ice on the lake should be thin enough to break apart in about a week's time. We will drag the lake to see if we can find anything regarding Bob and Jeff's death." He said this to her in a very sincere voice. "Thank you officers, it would be nice to have his ashes to hold on to. He left to quick I was only left with his personal belongings. I never got the chance to say a real good bye or bury him with the respect he deserved." Said Sylvia with tears in her eyes as the emotions of her husband being gone took over. "We will do the best we can Ma'am. If you need anything don't hesitate to give us a call." Said officer Sparrow as he handed her a card with both their names on it and contact numbers. The officers nodded to Julia and began walking away towards their cruiser. Sylvia closed the door and sat on the floor. Crying. Crying for her husband. Crying from sorrow and grief.

The weather was on Sylvia's side. It was sunnier and sunnier by the day and the ice was beginning to melt quick. The officer's stayed true to their word. Exactly a week from the day they told her the news they began dragging the lake. They went at it for 5 days straight. But the only thing they were able to find was debris of a plane and some garbage. No trace of John or Bob's remains. The police concluded that they will close the investigation as by now they assumed if the bodies had came back up in the time of the accident and floated to shore animals such as wolves would've dragged them on land and ate them up. They knew after dragging the lake that they elliminated all chances of finding their bodies. After telling

Sylvia the disappointing news, they made a report and presumed the gentleman dead.

Sylvia was heartbroken. She had come to terms with their death but the only hope she had left was that one day she would going to be able to see her husband again. Whether it was in the form of ashes or a casket. She just wanted to see him one last time. She had no choice but to go to court and declare Bob's death but was told she had to wait at least 3 years before she could make it legal. Financially, Sylvia was struggling. The bills were piling up day by day. She had $ 50,000 life insurance and after Bob's death all income disappeared. She had been living off their retirement savings while also selling her cupcakes at her cousin's bakery but she didn't make enough to pay all the bills with it let alone enough to survive. Sadly Sylvia had to sell the farm. She had no choice left. Thankfully the farm sold quickly. After just 3 days Sylvia got an offer for $100,000. She took it right away. A newlywed couple had bought the farm. They said it was the perfect place to start a family. Sylvia knew they were a good fit and that she was giving the land away to people who would appreciate it as much as her husband always did. Once the sale was finalized Sylvia decided to move to Pickton and start a new life for herself. She figured it was a home away from home. Perfect for starting a new life. Soon after Sylvia moved to Pickton, she decided to see Bob's mother. She wasn't doing too well with her health. Her old age was beginning to make her life harder by day. When she saw her she couldn't believe how much she had aged. She had pale skin, hardly any hair and she was as weak as a newborn baby. Even in her fragile state Sylvia knew it was only right to let her know of her sons death. She was worried that the news might kill her. A parent should never have to bury their child. And in this case, they didn't even have any remains left to bury. "Hello my darling" she said as she took her shaking hand out to greet Sylvia. "Hello mother! Oh it's so good to see you. I've missed you so much! How are you feeling?" Said Sylvia as she hugged her fragile body. She was as thin as a toothpick. "Oh you know, every day is a battle. Some days I'm strong and some days I can hardly move. You look so beautiful Sylvia. Gosh I would give anything to be your age again." She said with a very soft chuckle. "How are my sons? Have you heard anything? I dream about them sometimes you know. I have dreams of Bob being little and of Jeff playing with his red toy truck his father gave him for Christmas. I miss them so much Sylvia." "I've got some bad news for you darling. The policeman came to me a few months ago and told me that they would drag the lake to see if they could find their remains. But all they found was some garbage and dubris of a plane. They believe that they wolves may have eaten their remains. I'm so sorry mother." Said Sylvia as she put her arms around her and gave her a soft kiss on the cheek. "Well, I don't believe my sons are dead. And I refuse to believe it until I see their bodies." "I know, I find it hard to believe it myself some days. It gets really hard at times. I miss Bob's laugh, and kisses and the smell of his aftershave in the morning. There's not a day that goes by that I don't think of him. But I'm trying to be strong. Holding on to all the past memories was making every day harder and harder. I had to sell the farm because I couldn't afford to live on the land anymore. I sold it to a loving family that appreciated what they were buying. I've moved to Pickton two weeks ago. I figured I had to move on with my life if I had a chance of surviving this pain." Said Sylvia as she softly began to cry. "I know darling. It's going to be okay I promise you. Why don't you stay with me? I could surely use someone to take care of me. The nurse comes by every 3 days but it's getting harder and harder for me to change myself and do things around the house. And your company will heal my pain as well. We can get through this together." "Of course I will take care of you mother. You might be Bob's real mother but you became mine as well the day I married him." And with that, Sylvia moved in and began caring for Bob's mother. As days turned into weeks, Bob's mother took a turn for the worst. She had caught pneumonia and her body was not strong enough to survive it. The inevitable happened and she passed away 5 weeks later. Sylvia and Julie planned her funeral. And they made sure it was as beautiful as can be. The whole town came out to say their goodbye's. Sylvia and Julie said a prayer for Jeff and Bob that day as they closed the mother's casket. "May you see them up in heaven. May you be with your sons together again. May you all look out for all of us." They both said as they said their final good bye.

Julie had received the house as per her mother's will and a fair amount of money in the will. It was enough to put her through high school and allow her to set a life up for herself. Julie kept the inheritance and allowed Sylvia to continue living in her mother's home. It was the only way she could think of a proper thank you for taking such good care of her mother in her last couple of weeks.

Two weeks after Julie buried her mother, she was on her way home from a long day at school and decided to check the post office box on her way home. When she opened the box she saw a little box very neatly wrapped. There was no address except for J&B written in big bold letters. She put into her school bag and decided to open it when she got home. It was addressed to her. She was very puzzled and opened the box as soon as she got into her room. As she opened the box, she saw two pairs of white socks and a locket resting on top. She shreaked. It was the locket Sylvia had bought for Bob. The beautiful locket she once saw when her brother came home to show her on his 18th birthday. As she opened the locket she saw a picture of Jeff from his prom night and on the other side was the picture of Bob which was always kept there. But there was something different this time. The picture of Jeff was never in the locket. The locket contained a picture of Sylvia and Bob originally. This seemed very strange to Julie. She began pacing around the room trying to figure out what all of this meant. Was someone playing a horrible joke on her? And then she looked at the box again. B&J. Bob and Jeff! And it hit her like an ocean wave. They were alive! They were trying to tell her they were still alive! She dropped on the floor and began crying. Tears of joy, tears of sadness and she looked up to the sky and said "Thank you mother! Thank you! I know you had something to do with this!" She put the locket around her neck and decided to keep this to herself. She knew if the guys really wanted to have the world know they were alive they would not have went through such trouble with the clues. Julie felt comfort in her heart for the first time in over 2 years. She looked up at the moon that night and closed her eyes. "I hope the two of you are looking at this same moon right now. We will be together one day." The same day, in Ottawa the police still hadn't found who robbed the bank and with no money found at the lake that made them eliminate Bob and Jeff, so the cops began to search some new suspects. This made is easier for John and Grant especially given their new identities. But there was no way they could know this information.

Meanwhile John and Grant finally reached Vancouver. They decided to dump their car and buy another one. They settled with a 1953 Cadillac Coup Deville. The guys loved their new car. It was luxurious just like the way their lives were about to get. They decided to stay in a old motel for a couple of days called the "West Way Motel." The guys had both grown out a beard by now and had died their hair on the greyish side which made them look older. They also noticed, by the reaction of the women they tried to pick up, that the beard and grey hair made them less noticable. Not even the women seemed to be interested no matter what they said. They ate at some good restaurants but after 2 days they began getting very bored. "Man, I'm horny. I want some fun. It's hard picking up girls here. They're all so snobby and hard to get. I don't like that. No way I'm going to work hard for a woman I don't plan on making a wife." Said John as he plopped himself onto the bed. "Well take out the newspaper from the dresser cupboard. I'm sure there will be some ads for us. Vancouver is big on strippers." Said Grant with a wink.

"Hey you're right! There's a whole page here offering for some ladies to show us a good time for $100 for 2 hours of pleasure." Said John staring at the newspapers at the half naked women advertised. Grant made the call and sure enough an hour later, they had two Asian women show up. They were very busty and very put together. They walked in, and got straight to business. "I'm Alice, and this is Grishka. We like to get paid up front." John handed them $100 each and sat back and said "let's see what you got!" The women had turned on the radio and began to strip. They would twirl around in circles giving the guys a chance to view their full assets.

As soon as the girls took their clothes off, the guys had a hard on as big as Florida. They couldn't wait. The girls picked up on this and both began walking towards them. They each sat down on their laps and put their hands on their bare naked breasts. As soon as the guys felt their nipples it was game over and the fun really started. By the time the two hours were up John and Grant decided that they still didn't have enough fun and handed the girls another $100.00 to stay for another 2 hours. The girls took the money and didn't object. The had spent another

2 hours with the guys and a couple of more rounds. When the time was up, the girls got dressed said goodnight and the guys went to bed happy after getting their stones off.

Next day, when they woke up they decided to buy some better clothes then what they had. It was time to clean up a little. They also needed nice suits for the big business meeting in B.C. they wanted to be taken seriously. They went back to the motel and dumped the old clothes into the garbage. It was now time to move on. The guys picked themselves up some nice suits, and ties to make sure their look showed that they were ready for business. The next morning they jumped into their car and headed north it was about an hour north of Prince Rupert. Once they got there they decided to check into the "Ace Motel." After they settled in, they began working on their plan. They decided to call it an early night so that they could be well rested for their meeting with Christopher tomorrow. But first things first. They got two bank accounts. One for each brother so that everything would look normal. They figured about $25,000 in each account was not out of place since most people coming there were basically business people looking to buy. So that afternoon they established these credits at the bank and it went smoothly.

The next day they put on their best suits, hopped into their car and headed down to the resort. Christopher was waiting in his office for them. He was dressed in a very sharp suit. He stood up from his seat and extended his hand to the gentleman. "Hello! My name is Christopher, it's such a pleasure to finally meet you." He said with a very kind voice. "Hello Chris, my name is Grant and this is my brother John. We have been looking forward to meeting you for weeks. So glad to finally be here." Said Grant as he firmly shook Christopher's hand and then John followed with a handshake as well. "Well I thought that before we talk business I would take you around the resort and show you around. We have a ton of construction going on everywhere but it's only fair to let you know what you're working with before you decide on any big investment decisions." Said Chris as he began putting on his beige coat that must have cost a fortune. "That would be great Chris. After you" Said Grant following Christopher outside with John right behind him. The place was huge. And really nice. Construction was going on literally everywhere. Roads were being fixed, buildings were being repainted, new sidewalks were getting put in. "This land is good for about 10,000 people after we put up all the buildings and shops. But it's definitely a great investment. We have done a couple of research studies with the folks in this town and based on our results we expect to be at max capacity within 3 months of opening and that should be a current average for the year as we can accommodate people with activities in all seasons throughout the year." Said Christopher with a sense of pride. Blood began rushing in Grant's veins. He could smell money and he could smell a lot of it. The fact that Christopher seemed very into this project and was very educated in the field gave him a sense of relief as well. "Over here, we plan to open a few motels, variety stores, a black smith shop and right over there we will have a path where the horses will pull buggy's with the tourists so that they can explore the mountains during the summer season." He said as he pointed to the hill side that was covered in large amounts of dirt from all the machines working on building proper pathways. "This place is very classy!" said John as he saw the gigantic sign with big bold letters that were shining in bright lights that said "Happy Resort" "Thank you John, our key to success is to keep our customers happy so they have reasons to want to come back every year if not more than once a year. Our focus is the children as well. When kids have a great time they want to come back over and over again. Of course the adults are important as well, but a couple of studies have shown that a lot of people come back when they see their kids had a great time." "That's very smart thinking!" Said Grant intrigued with the knowledge he was already gaining from Christopher.

They followed Christopher back into his office to discuss their investment plans. "Christopher, Grant and I decided that we will split up into two businesses. We prefer to have our own projects going on." Said John as he began the meeting. "Great! What type of shops were you thinking of purchasing?" Said Christopher as he pulled out a pen and paper ready to begin. "Grant would like to set up a restaurant. He's a phenomenal cook, plus he likes to work with the ladies." Said John with a wink. "And I would like to set up a sport shop." "Sounds great guys, well Grant, based on the restaurant I think what would be ideal for you is this point on the map right here." Said Christopher as he took out a map of the resort. "It is located on the lake in the middle of resort. For this amount of space, you would need a $15,000 down payment and if everything goes well we can close the deal in 3 days. And as far you John, I think this area would be great for sport shop. It's a walking distance from Grant's restaurant and it's right beside the slope. For this amount of space I would only need a $10,000 down payment." The guys set back and considered these offers in silence. After about 2 minutes they both decided with a solid handshake with Christopher that they agreed. And so their new journey began.

John had an easier time opening up the sport shop. He repainted the place and had the shop running in two weeks. Grant opened up about two weeks later. It was easy to get staff because people were coming in in droves as soon as it advertised in Vancouver, Prince Rupert and also in the States. Lots of people wanted to move there. Either to retire or just to work. The place would be in full motion in months. And by god, they were right. They couldn't keep up with visitors, they would make tons of money in no time! As the resort became sold out and the hospital opened up, things were in full swing. They even had to start building more motels as the resort was getting too busy for the upcoming winter season. Which was great for John's sport store.

And finally when winter was upon them business was great for both brothers. Grant was just in his glory with his staff and had about 10 beautiful waitresses. He didn't know which one was going to be his favourite. He kept on teasing John about them. And John would go eat at the restaurant on regular basis and would do his share of flirting with the waitresses as well. And so a little brotherly competition began. One night they decided to flip a coin as to which one would get who. Everything was going very well for the both of them. As things started to look up for the guys they began thinking that

now was perhaps time to begin thinking about settling down. And so a few days later they started to make passes at some waitresses. And the girls loved every minute of it. Since the two were very handsome and friendly. One night they invited two of their favourite girls to the Grant's cottage he had built. John had Karen and Grant had Susan. Both were striking blondes, about 5 feet tall with nice asses and not to forget the top parts. First they had a couple of cocktails at the restaurant, closed the place up and away they went to Grant's cottage. The ladies were surprised at how Grant kept his place so clean. Nothing extravagant as far as furniture or anything but looked like a happy place. They had a few more cocktails and the girls knew what was expected of them. After a couple of glasses of wine, John asked Karen to go next door to his place. And she gracefully accepted. Once there, he put soft music on and willingly started to tease. John stood up and began dancing with her and they were very close to each other. She began bringing her thigh up to John's crotch. And guess what. It's fun time from there. About 20 minutes of that and they were both on the rug on the floor teasing each other. Clothes off, she was gently stroking his testicles to John's delight. That he blew his load on the spot. But he was good for a second shot at it anyway. He promptly got down on her licking her clitoris. She was screaming with joy. So much so that even the neighbours could hear her. And of course not to be outdone Grant had similar ideas. He started on Susan. Pretty much the same way. The girls were so satisfied they fell asleep about an hour later. The boys were so proud and happy that they woke the girls up for an early breakfast and a little morning go. It was just heavenly for all. Once they finished with pleasure off to work they went and that whole day you could see Karen and Susan chit chat about their tryst the night before. Grant was also smiling all day and why not this was probably going to be a hit for them. Maybe even a life time deal. The next day things cooled off for a couple of days everyone was happy hoping for a return match. And a return match they got. 3 days later. Which happened to be the weekend anyway.

They all decided to make plan a little trip to Vancouver. Grant had trained one of the girls to manage the place for when he wanted a day off. And John was also training one guy to run his sports store for when he was off. Everything was set up for the weekend. They took off Saturday morning with their girls for the big city. Once they got there they got two motel rooms side by side and went for lunch. Nice steak and lobster with wine. They were just like kids again. Very happy and playful. They were in love. They went visiting the beautiful marina. They saw beautiful exotic fish, sharks even a whale. And that took most of the day. They came back to the motel. Grant suggested that he would go to get some wine at the liquor store and got 3 bottles of wine. The boys were so in love with the women, they decide to propose the idea of having them move in with them. The girls both agreed which ended up calling for a little party. John and Grant set up a nice little surprise party at Grant's cottage. They had a lot of fun, they invited a few people they knew at the restaurant and sports store. About 20 people showed up and the party was on. It turned out really good. Now that the fun was over it was time to get more serious. As time went by, the girls gave birth to two gorgeous little boys that they were extremely proud of. And so life went on, Sylvia had a new husband a couple more kids by now.

Business was never any better at this point. A couple more years went by the kids were growing fast. Just about old enough to go to school. It's now winter again. It snowed a lot this winter. The ski hills were just dandy. But it snowed a little too much and the mountains became a hazard due to the risk of avalanches. They started to put signs up to be extremely careful of their skiing. However that didn't faze John of Grant. They were average skiers. By now it was a Sunday afternoon, January 5th, 1961. John and Grant decided to go skiing. It was sunny and cold. The snow sparkled with the sun shining at its surface. Away they go. Everything was just dandy until about

4 pm. They heard some rumbling up the mountain. As they turned to look, here it was coming about 50 miles an hour. Straight down on them. They were too far up the hill. They were going to get hit for sure. They tried to beat it down but the avalanche was way too fast for them. They got hit from behind and were pushed down about a 100 yards. And guess what. There was an old shack there. They were holding hands and luckily got buried by the shack. Which sort of protected them from being killed. They had about 4 feet of snow on top of them. They managed to dig themselves out enough to get air. After about 30 minutes everything sort of cooled down a bit. The avalanche had stopped and they managed to get in the shack. They were bruised severally. Grant had a broken thumb and John had very sore ribs. But happy to be alive. Within a couple of hours help was on the way. Helicopters were there to help with the rescue as well. They spotted John and Grant waving by the shack. They immediately went to their rescue. Once in the helicopter, they were rushed to the hospital which was small. The doctor immediately looked after them. He put them to bed for observation overnight. He advised their girlfriends they were okay and they were allowed to come visit them. The girls were so happy they cried for half an hour. But the next morning in abundance a photographer of the town came snapping pictures of the

guys as they were leaving the hospital. They began taking pictures of them and asking for them to share their story. Even before John and Grant realized that this would hit the news. They got nervous and decided to make a run for it into their cars. They went directly to Grant's cottage and discuss what they were going to do. They talked to their girlfriends for a bit and told them that they should go away for a few days because they didn't like publicity. They said they were shy and couldn't handle it. And of course the girls believed them because they never lied to them before. So they told the girls they would be back in a week when things cooled off. They grabbed their hidden money where they kept in the outhouse stashed under the wooden floor. They jumped into one car, kissed their girlfriend's goodbye and told them not to worry. They told them to look after their businesses while they were gone. And away they went. They had to move fast before these pictures hit the papers and television. They figured they had time to hit the border before daylight. They should be halfway to Mexico by noon the next day. If they both continuously drive. The next day they were passed Seattle. Now it was time to buy another car and ditch the old one. They proceeded to a junk yard and asked how much they could get for a coup de ville which had lots of miles. They attendant told them $100. And not to look too devious, they had taken their plates off and thrown them away just before going in. Off they go to a dealer next store and purchase a 1957 Ford Fair lane. Got new plates, Canadian ones and away they go. They wanted to be in Mexico the next day. They would have to really move to make it. They would stop at McDonald's for a fast meal and run. Luck was on their side, back at happy resort people were so busy digging out the dead from the avalanche nobody paid any attention. There was a death toll of about 8 people. So there wasn't too much attention put on them yet. Their girlfriends told people coming around that the boys didn't like publicity and took a few days to rest. The next day they were now at the boarder of Mexico starting to get nervous as hell. But to their amazement the border guards asked them where they were going and they told them they were on their way to Mexico City for a vacation. No questions asked, the guard told them to enjoy themselves. And john said to Grant what a relief again! So they decided to drive a little further and grab a motel. They wanted to rest and discuss the next move over a bottle of tequila. So they drove another 3 hours to a nice little town. They got a motel, grabbed a few hours' sleep, had a nice shower and grabbed some breakfast. Then they grabbed a newspaper to see if anything was mentioned about the avalanche. Not even a word on it. Good news!

Where do we settle down this time? They got a map of all the resorts around Mexico city. Lots of places were available for rent. So they decided to check around for anything to buy. Maybe a nice little hotel near the beach. Might do the trick. They didn't want to waste too much time doing nothing.

Back in Ottawa, this detective in charge of the original bank heist and disappearance who he happened to see in the national news and to his dismay saw the picture of the two survivors of the avalanche. And just about dropped dead by the surprise. Because he happened to be the one who married Sylvia. After she got the death certificate of her ex nobody else paid at the station paid any attention as to the resemblance of the two boys and his wife also saw the pictures and didn't know if her husband had seen them. By the way his name is Dan. When Dan got home that night he didn't know what to expect from Sylvia. Does she know or doesn't she? But he knew by the expression on her face that she did. He gave her a big hug and kiss and asked her for a beer. And she gladly obliged. They sat down to talk about this serious problem. Dan although he was a tough cop, he was also very diplomatic in his ways when it comes to tough situations like this. So he said to her "I guess you know what is going on" "yes, I saw the news. The news broadcast today."

And they decided to discuss this problem very carefully. Nobody at the station recognized the two so he said "look honey, we have two beautiful kids. Maybe we shouldn't jeopardise our lives or the kids. And the interest money you got plus our marriage. This could ruin our lives. Why don't we just carry on and now even think about it. Only their sister Julie might have seen their news. Why don't you call her to see if she knows anything about it. To their surprise Julie finally admitted that she already knew they were alive. In happy resort they had the funeral for the 20 people who died and they were slowly getting back to normal. Now the police, still scratching their heads as to what happened to Grant and john, there seemed to be no trace past Vancouver. And still a mystery. Ottawa was a different story. Dan and his wife and Julie sort of admired the two for their heroic deeds. And they kept it to themselves. As the story goes, the two boys Grant & John got a job on a ship unknown to anyone and disappeared somewhere in Europe never to heard of again.

Printed in Canada